Through Her Eyes

Revised 2nd Edition

Copyright © 2012 by Krystol

ISBN- 13:978-0615597294

ISBN-10: 0615597297

No part of this book can be reproduced, transmitted, or stored in whole or part by any means, including graphic, electronic, or mechanical without the express written consent of the publisher except in the case of brief quotations embodied in critical articles or reviews.

Through Her Eyes

This is a work of fiction. The events and characters described here and imaginary and are not intended to refer to specific places or living persons.

Published by: Krystol Diggs Publishing

Written by: Krystol

Edited by: Shonell Bacon

Cover Design by: Deatri King-Bey

Through Her Eyes

A Novel by

Krystol

Dedication:

I dedicate this book to my grandmother's Gloria and Shirley. Although you have both passed on I still hold the love, and knowledge that you both have shown me close to my heart. I thank god to have gotten to known both of you. You may be gone but definitely not forgotten. With Love,

Krystol aka Tinnie Boo

Acknowledgments

To my grandmother, this book is for you. Thank you for instilling in me courage and the wisdom that anything is possible.

To my brother who is no longer here Michael, I miss you dearly and I thank you for always protecting me and showing me that I had to walk my own path.

To my great grandmother Anna who is no longer here, I thank you for teaching me that self perseverance is the key to life. You are truly missed.

To my cousin Bingo who is no longer here, I thank you for teaching me how to be independent and not lean on anyone. You are truly missed.

To my mother Cheryl I thank you for what you have done for me, for allowing me to follow my heart and being there for me even when you couldn't be; you instilled in me courage and faith.

Also I want to thank you for being the great mother that I knew you could be. To my father Brian, I thank you for protecting me from the world, and although you still do that, it is time for me to fly on my own. I also thank you for loving me and being the great father that you are.

Through Her Eyes

To my aunt Debbie, I love you so much and I
appreciate your support.

To my brother B, although we always lived in different
households, every time I needed you, you were there.
Thank you for taking the time to listen to me about
the men I dealt with, well the boys I dealt with.

To my cousins Eric and Ericka thank you for being
there for me when I need you. Without you guys, I
have no idea sometimes what I could have gone
through. I love you.

To my aunt Terry and cousin Shannon, thank you for
being there for me. Aunt Terry, thank you for keeping
me in check when I needed it the most. Shannon,
thanks for listening when I needed to talk and giving
me great advice. You can't beat me up anymore!

To the bullies who teased and humiliated me
throughout my years in school, I also want to you
thank you for making me strong.

To the teachers that I have had over the years, I want
to thank you for pushing me and letting me know that
I can do what I put my mind to. This is not the end
but only the beginning for me.

I would also like to give a special shout out to my

author friends: K.D Harris, Larissa Robinson, Madison, Ericka McCoy, Deatri-King Bey, Laura T.Johnson, Terry L Wroten, Judy Richburg, Nicole Shelton, Jamila E.Gomez, La Smith,Barbara Grovner, and everyone else that I may forget, I am truly sorry, but I thank you. To my groups that I am apart of Urban Forum, All4one, Bookaholics, Diamond Eyes Book Club and many more. I thank you all for the support.

The Prelude

I knew that my life was going to be tough, coming out of the womb three months early and living to tell about it. It was December 18th on a Monday afternoon, and my mom Jackie, was cooking fried fish, fried potatoes and corn. Wearing her blue striped maternity shirt and pants to match, Jackie left the kitchen to answer the ringing phone.

"Hello."

"What you doing?" my dad, Demetrius said.

"Cooking dinner for you when you get off work."

My parents weren't married, but they were together for the sake of me.

"I'll see you when I get home."

"Alright," Jackie said, hanging up the phone and going back into the kitchen to turn over the fish. Jackie started to feel some pressure in her stomach. She spoke to her stomach, "I know you're hungry. I am, too." She continued to finish cooking dinner until the pressure in her stomach worsened. She sat on her burgundy recliner and began rubbing her belly. There wasn't any pain, but the baby was moving a lot. Jackie got comfortable in the chair and ended up falling asleep.

Two hours later she woke up to intense pain in her stomach. She jumped up in fear and looked down to see blood on the chair. She grabbed the phone and called 911. Then she called her mother, Shug, and told her the situation and that she was on her way to the hospital.

Shug said in a panic, "I'll meet you at the hospital!"

As the paramedics rolled Jackie into the hospital through the double doors, all she heard was, "...woman pregnant and she is hemorrhaging. The baby may not make it. We have to save the mother."

"What is going on, what is wrong with my baby?" Jackie yelled.

The doctor responded, "Ma'am, we are trying to find out."

Shug came into the room and held her hand and told her Demetrius was on his way. All of a sudden, pain rushed through Jackie's body. The doctor raced into the room and checked her blood pressure.

"Her BP is up really high. We are going to have to get this baby out now." Then he said to Shug, "Miss, you are going to have to wait in the waiting room."

"You can't take the baby out. I am only six months

pregnant!" Jackie said, breathing heavily.

"You could die if we don't deliver now! Jackie, I know that you're in pain, but I need you to count backwards from ten."

"Ten, nine, eight, seven..." She was out cold before she made it to six.

When Jackie opened her eyes, she saw Shug and Demetrius sitting next to her.

"We have a baby girl and she weighs one pound," Demetrius said with a smile.

Demetrius sat in the NICU with me while I was in the incubator. The nurses had to feed me through a tube and I wasn't breathing on my own. After a week, Jackie finally went to see me. They hadn't picked out a name yet because they didn't know my chances of survival. Everyone was coming to the hospital to see me with toys and stuffed animals. The newspaper even came to do a story. My mom held my tiny hand and just cried.

"Demetruis, is she going to make it?"

"I pray for her every day I come to see her."

The next day the doctor spoke with Jackie and my dad about my condition.

"Mr. and Mrs. Woodard, she still isn't breathing on

her own and I need to know what the next step is."
They didn't want me to suffer, so they decided to pull
the plug and let me rest in peace. Jackie cried
hysterically as she slowly walked down the hall to my
room. I was laying there with my eyes closed
breathing with the monitor.

The doctor grabbed and pulled the plug. Jackie
started crying so loud that the other nurses could hear
her. Everyone said a prayer over me when all of a
sudden, my cries interrupted the prayer.

The doctor spoke. "Wow, it's a miracle! Excuse me; I
need to check her to see if she is okay. Everyone, this
is a miracle! Your baby girl is breathing on her own."

"Thank you, my baby's eyes are open and she is
breathing. We will name her Melanie, Melanie
Woodard," Jackie said, now smiling.

I never got tired of Shug telling me that story. Every
time she told it to me, it nearly made tears form in my
eyes.

Three months later, I was able to go home with my
family. When I went home, I weighed five pounds.
My family was there to greet me for my homecoming.
Despite my size, despite the fact that I almost didn't
make it, that not even my parents could trust me to

live by my very own breath, I knew that I was put on this earth for a reason. I was a survivor. I was meant to be here and see the world, even if I wanted to come three months early. I was here to stay.

Chapter 1

By the time I was ten years old, there were a lot of changes in my life. The most drastic of them was Jackie starting to use drugs. As a result I had to move in with my grandmother, Shug, and I only saw my dad on the weekends. My dad wasn't always there, but he was there when it counted.

"Melanie, are you all packed and ready to go?" Shug asked.

"Yes, Mum Mum, I'm ready."

"Okay, because I think I see your dad's car coming."

I raced down the stairs with my bag on my back. I looked out the window and sighed. "Damn, that's the neighbor's car." The horn of their blue Grand Am always sounded like a duck. While I was waiting for Dad to arrive, I grabbed "The Color Purple", which I had to read for school. I saw the movie a thousand and one times, but the book was way better. Just as I was getting into my favorite part, Shug's hollering bought me out of my trance. "Melanie, your crazy father is here."

He walked in the door. His 6'2" frame nearly took up the entire doorway. When our eyes connected, he gave me his best toothpaste commercial smile. My father was the definition of perfect in my book. From his smooth milk chocolate skin, baby face, to his jet black curly hair. He was what I dreamed of in a man. I always wanted to be with a man who was similar to my father.

"Hey Mum Mum."

"Hey Demetrius."

He walked over and kissed her on the cheek.

He then came over to me and wrapped his muscular arms around me. I knew his cologne would be trapped in my clothes. Sometimes that was all I had of him.

"You ready to go?"

"Yup, I just have to put my book away."

"What were you reading?"

"The Color Purple."

"The Color Purple, why are you reading that when you know the whole movie by heart?"

"Dad, it's for school."

"Okay, I was just asking," he said letting out a laugh.

I gave Shug a hug then left the house with my dad and got into his car.

When my dad got into the car he said, "We are going to Grandma Shirley's for awhile."

"She playing cards with the family?"

"You know it."

I looked forward to going to Grandma Shirley's house. I would get to spend time with my dad's side of the family. Most of all I loved to watch everyone play pitty pat while Grandma Shirley cussed them out 'cause she just knew they were cheating. My Grandma Shirley was the best. She had the prettiest chestnut brown complexion and a smile that would light up a room. But she didn't take no stuff, especially if you would try to cheat her in pitty pat.

She would smile at them all with that sweet innocent smile, while the whole time she was looking at all the players to see how many were cheating. She would cuss them out and then kick them out while winning their money. If she took their money, they'd still come back the next day to try to redeem themselves, but good luck with that. When we pulled up to the house, I saw my brother Q and my cousin Blair. As soon as my dad went into the house, I got hit in the back and neck.

"Stop playing all the time, y'all."

"Shut up," they both said.

"No, you shut up."

Q picked me up and slammed me on the grass while Blair pounced on me.

"Ouch, y'all play too much!"

"Mel, be quiet. That don't even hurt," Blair said.

"It does so!"

"Y'all better leave that baby alone!" My grandma yelled from the door.

Once I was done being bullied by Q and Blair, I went inside and, like usual, the infamous card game was going on. At the table there was my dad, my grandma, my other brother Terron and the neighbors, Mr. Steve and Ms. Pauline. I pulled up a chair next to my grandma to sit and watch. There was alcohol all over the table; you name it, it was there. E and J, Christian Brothers, Miller Lite, and Bacardi, with the chasers Sprite and Pepsi.

"Now Melanie, you see these deuces in my hand?" my grandma asked.

"Yes."

"These are wild which means they go with anything, okay?"

"Shirley, pay attention to the game, we playing for money," my grandma's boyfriend, Homie, yelled from the kitchen.

"Mother fucker, I am watching the game! You stay your black ass in the kitchen. You ain't even playing anyway."

Everyone in the room laughed so hard 'cause she cussed Homie out then went back to the game like he didn't say anything.

Three hours later, it was time for everyone to leave. Ms. Pauline was drunk, so Terron, Blair, Q, Taya, and I had to help her get home. It was always the family routine to come over Grandma Shirley's house to play cards.

Then suddenly, things started to change.

The card games moved to my dad and Ms. Sugar's house. I didn't like Sugar at first because I felt that she was trying to take my dad away from me. At the time I didn't know any better.

My dad and Ms. Sugar eventually got married. I didn't want them to only because I knew that once they got married, I wouldn't see my dad as much as I did, and he would have a new family with Sugar and her two children, Mart and Eddie. I started to think about the talk my dad and I had before the wedding started.

"Mel."

"Yes, Daddy."

"Do you really like Sugar?"

"I don't know. If I say no, you're still going to marry her anyway."

"Baby, tell Daddy how you feel," he said, putting his hand on my shoulder.

"Dad, she is taking me away from you." I crossed my arms across my chest.

"No, she isn't, Mel. I am still going to be your father. You do understand that, don't you?"

"Yes."

"I'm going to marry Sugar and we are still going to hang out all the time just like we do now."

"You promise?"

"I promise."

"Ok. Does that mean that I can live with you now?" I said with a huge smile.

That smile immediately faded when I caught my father's expression.

"Now, sweetie, there isn't enough room at my house for you, and I really think that living with your grandma is the best thing for you."

"I understand," I said totally disappointed.

"Good, I love you, Boop."

"I love you, too, Daddy."

I felt like everyone was looking at me even though they were staring at the bride and groom. Even at ten years old, I could see what my dad must have seen. Sugar was a very beautiful, cinnamon skinned woman. She was definitely filling out her wedding dress in all the right places. Once the vows were said, I felt like my life was forever changed. I wanted to move in with my dad, but that wasn't happening. I felt unwanted because my father didn't want me to live with him. I started crying because I felt like I had to give him up. But that wasn't the case at all; I just didn't understand the concept of marriage.

The day after the wedding the loneliness and sadness I felt grew to unimaginable pain. I was at Shug's house playing double dutch with my friends when Shug called me in the house, "Melanie, come get the phone. It's your dad."

"Okay, Mum Mum."

I walked in the house and picked up the phone.

"Hey Daddy."

"Hey Boop, I have some bad news about grandma."

He was trying to keep from breaking down while he was on the phone with me. I was sitting in the chair, playing with the red barrette I had in my hair.

"Daddy, I know she is sick, but she said she was getting better for me."

"Baby, Grandma died today."

The news had blindsided me and the tears immediately fell.

"Aaawwww baby, it's okay to cry, okay?"

"Why did she have to die? Now I'm not going to be able to go over her house anymore and watch the card games or help her cook."

"I know, baby, but we are going to be alright, okay? Daddy has to hang up the phone now. I will call you later."

"Ok, Daddy."

As soon as I got off the phone, Shug came and hugged me. The more she consoled me, the more hysterically I cried.

"Mum Mum, it's not fair that she had to die!"

"I know, sweetie, but everyone has to die one day, even you and I. It's a part of life, and I know you will miss her."

"Yes I will, very much." I said sniffling.

I could picture the last time I saw her. She was laying in a hospital bed in her living room.

"Hey Grandma."

"Hey Sweetie Pie."

Her voice was so soft that I could barely hear what she was saying. I sat next to her bed in a chair.

"Grandma, I can't wait until you're all better so you can play cards and we can cook dinners again."

"Yeah, that would be nice, sweetie pie. But if we can't do those things anymore, remember the good times we had, okay?"

She started coughing so hard that my dad had to give her some water through a straw. Seeing my grandma sick like that made me afraid because I couldn't picture life without her. Her coughing stopped as she sipped the water. After my dad made sure she was alright, we got ready to leave.

"Boop, you ready to go?"

"Yes Daddy."

"Grandma, I'll be back soon to come visit again. I love you."

"I love you, too, sweetie pie."

I leaned over and kissed her on the cheek. She smiled at me then closed her eyes and drifted off to sleep. If I had known that was going to be the last time I would see her, I would have stayed longer.

✳✳✳✳✳

Through Her Eyes

The day of my grandmother's funeral I remembered how crowded the church was. There were barely enough seats to accommodate everyone. I sat with Q and Blair. Watching everyone cry and scream in pain for her made me cry even harder. I thought of all the times I watched her play cards, and how I helped her cook dinners. I just wanted to crawl into a little hole and never come back out. Everyone was hugging and kissing me on my cheeks asking if I was okay. How could I be okay, I was ten years old seeing my grandma in a casket?

It was time for me to go up and view my grandmother's body for the last time. I looked at her in her light pink dress with her jet black wig. When I touched her hand, I noticed that it was cold. I quickly pulled my hand back and ran up to my dad. I buried my head in his chest as he bent down and hugged me. After the funeral everyone went to my grandma's house for the repast. I sat in my grandmother's rocking chair, silent. My stepbrother Mart asked me if I wanted anything to eat and I didn't answer him. Then Q picked me up and I started crying again.

"It's okay, Tinky," Q said. "I am here, okay?" My dad's side of the family called me Tinky because I was a preemie.

As the days went on, I missed my grandmother more and more. I still couldn't accept the fact that she was gone.

✳✳✳✳✳

One day I was outside playing with my friends when I saw my neighbor Josh sitting on the porch with Jackie and Shug. Josh was nineteen and I had a crush on him. Josh would come over and play video games with me and take me to the park from time to time. He always asked for Shug's permission and because she trusted him, we were always allowed to go. We would play on the swings and he would watch me play with other kids.

That same week on a Wednesday morning, Shug got dressed to go out to the outlets and then to the casino which she did often. Jackie was sleeping in the room and she was supposed to be watching me. I was downstairs playing my video game when I heard a knock on the door. I knew never to answer the door for strangers.

"Who is it?" I asked.

"Josh."

I opened the door and saw Josh's smiling face.

"Hey, Mel," he said, "who is here with you?"

"My mom is, but she is sleeping."

I sat back in the chair where I was playing my video game. Josh asked if he could play the game with me. I restarted the fighting game and put it on two players so that he could play, too. I was happy that I had someone to play with because I hated playing by myself.

Two hours later both Josh and I were still playing the game, trying to beat the highest score. We were almost at the final level of the game when Josh stopped the game and kissed me on the lips.

I had a puzzled look on my face and said, "Eeeww, why did you do that?"

"I like you, Mel. Don't you like me?" Josh responded too casually.

I was terrified. I immediately knew that the kiss wasn't right at all. Josh sensed the fear in my eyes and smiled devilishly. Swiftly, he got up from the chair, carried me to the couch, and placed his hand over my mouth tightly.

Tears streamed from my eyes. Josh then placed his free hand on my breast. I tried to break free from him, but he was too strong. I even tried to scream for

Jackie, but his hand was gripped too tight.

Josh then placed his hand on my vagina and roughly inserted two fingers inside of me. I cried out from the pain. Josh was looking at my face, smiling like he was enjoying it. Finally I got the strength to bite his hand. When I bit his hand, he jumped up and yelled. "You bitch." Then he ran out of the house. I sat up from the couch and it was wet because I had peed on myself. Quickly I ran upstairs screaming to Jackie, crying hysterically.

In the bedroom, I pushed on Jackie to wake her up. She didn't move from her sleep. I kept pushing and pushing, screaming, "Mom, wake up, wake up."

"Mel, what's wrong? Why are you crying?" Jackie said in fear.

I couldn't speak clearly trying to tell her what Josh did to me. She told me to calm down and tell her what happened. I told her everything that Josh did. She got up from the bed and put on her clothes to go next door to see if Josh was home.

As Jackie went to Josh's house, Shug walked in and saw me crying.

"What's going on? Shug asked. "Why are you crying, Melanie?"

I told her what happened, and Shug quickly called the cops.

She hugged me and told me that everything was going to be okay.

"Ok, Mum Mum," I managed to say.

Jackie came back in the house and was talking to Shug about what happened. As they were talking about the ordeal, the cops knocked on the door. Shug explained to the cops what happened. The officer asked to speak to me. I came downstairs and reiterated what Shug told them.

"Why didn't you hear the knock on the door?" the officer asked. "How could you leave a little girl downstairs by herself?"

Jackie explained to the officer that she was sleeping and didn't hear anything. The officer looked at her and shook his head in disgust. Terron walked in the house after seeing the cops' car in front of the house. Jackie told Terron what happened to me.

"What the fuck? I'm going to kill him."

"Now, Terron, calm down, we called the cops."

"Fuck calling the damn cops. While mom was sleep from smoking that damn crack, my sister was being molested. Naw, Mum Mum, I'm 'bout to go fuck him up right now."

"Terron, I said calm down," Shug repeated with a little more bass.

"Thank God Melanie had the nerve to do something. If not, my sister would have been raped instead of molested." Terron punched the wall and stormed out the house.

Later that night I was sitting in the bath tub, playing with my Barbie dolls when Jackie came in and sat on the toilet. With tears streaming down her face, she said, "Baby, I am so sorry that I wasn't awake to protect you."

"It's okay, Mommy."

"No it's not, baby, I am your mother and mothers are supposed to protect their children."

"Mommy."

"Yes, baby."

"What's crack?"

My mom started crying even harder. "Where did you hear that word from?"

"Terron was upset and I heard him say you were sleeping from smoking crack."

"Crack is something that I never want you to do. It's not good for you."

"Well, Mommy, if it's not good for you, then why are you smoking it?"

"Melanie, play with your dolls, okay Sweetie? I will be back to wash you up." She could barely finish her sentences.

After I had taken my bath, I was lying in the bed, trying to get rest like Shug told me. Jackie came running upstairs to me, still crying and apologizing for not being there for me. I just lay in the bed and listened to her. Then she said, "Mel, don't tell your dad what happened because if you do, he will go to jail. You don't want your dad to go to jail, do you? If your dad finds out about this he will kill Josh and they will send him to jail."

"No, Mommy," I said, shaking my head from side to side. "I don't want daddy to go to jail."

✳✳✳✳✳

Several months went by and I never saw Josh again. I didn't know what happened to him, if he went to jail or not. I still didn't tell my dad anything about what happened. Jackie and Shug kept a close eye on me at all times. I wasn't allowed to be outside without someone on the porch watching me. My family bought all these toys and new video games to keep me occupied. For me things were back to normal again. Sometimes I would have nightmares about what Josh did to me, but I never told anyone. Eventually they faded away and I was sleeping better. I learned early on what it was like to have to be strong and be willing to move forward no matter what happened.

Chapter 2

From elementary through high school, I was teased for being dark skinned, smart, not having the latest fashion; you name it, I was ridiculed for it. I would be in class taking a test and I would hear, "Melanie think she all that because she gets good grades with her ugly self. She don't even wear name brand clothes." I would sit there sometimes on the verge of tears, but I always said to myself, "Never let them see you cry."

To help me cope, Shug always told me that the bullies were jealous of me. Little did she know that it was I who was the jealous one. One day I was walking down the hall by myself and all the popular kids were in a crowd. I was in deep thought when this girl walked by me and said, "Bitch, move out my way. Girl, look at her, and she had the nerve to speak to me in math class. Ugh, I only talk to people who are popular. She is beneath me."

Beneath her, I thought, who the hell did she think she was? I couldn't just keep quiet this time, I mean not only was she ignorant, but she was insulting me. "Excuse me!"

The girl turned around as she rolled her eyes.

"What!" she screamed.

"First of all who are you calling a bitch, and second who do you think you are saying I am beneath you, when both our moms go get their food stamps on the same day."

"Ugh, no she didn't," her flunkie who was standing with her said.

"Yes, I did. You think you're better than everyone else 'cause you are mixed, but you ain't no better than the next person."

"Whatever," the girl said walking away

I was in chemistry class (which I didn't like that much, but I tried my best) listening to the teacher's lecture when a student shouted out, "Hey Melanie, when you turn out the lights, I bet people can't see you."

Everyone was laughing at me.

"Why are your pants so short? Ay y'all, Melanie is ready for the flood!"

The whole class erupted in laughter when the teacher told them to settle down. I ran out the classroom and into the girls' room. I didn't cry although I wanted to. Once I got home that day, just like every day, I would go to my room and speak with God.

"Why is everyone always teasing me? God, why did

you make me this way, why couldn't I be a lighter-skinned child? A richer child?" I cried those words until my eyes were red and puffy.

Later that night, while in bed, I stared up at the ceiling for what seemed like hours, trying to think of some positivity about my school situation but couldn't find any. I was willing to make friends, but as I was finding out, people didn't reciprocate. I made up my mind right then and there that I would tune the bullies out. I was determined to make friends and had some newfound confidence that I would. After a few more shadows danced on my ceiling from the cars outside, I felt my eyes getting heavy. Then the next thing I knew I was out like a light.

The next day at school I felt a whole lot better than I did the day before. I was trying my hardest to stay positive amongst my peers. The day was dragging along, which caused me to periodically look at the clock in each period I was in. The lone bright spot for me was Jazz, who was a loner like me. As lunch period was about to start, I caught up to her in the hallway.

"Hey Jazz."

"Hey Mel."

"We studying for the math test today?"

"Yea, we can do that."

"Sit with me at lunch."

"Okay, Mel," Jazz said, gave me a hug and then turned to walk away.

Lunch time came and Jazz and I were sitting at the table as planned.

"Okay Jazz, where should we start?"

"Let's start at the periodic table," she said opening her math book.

"Okay."

While we were sitting at the table studying, I heard someone say, "Wow, look at the nerds studying. How cute."

"Mel, let's just ignore them and keep studying," Jazz said touching my hand.

"Jazz, if you don't mind, can we study over the phone tonight? I'm just not feeling this right now."

"Okay, Melanie. Make sure you call me later."

"Okay Jazz," I said, walking away from the lunch table as fast as I could.

When I arrived in the guidance counselor's office, I did my usual and sat down in the chair, looking around. I swore she was my shrink.

"Melanie, tell me, what is bothering you today? Why

did you run out of the classroom the other day?"

"Because I am tired of being teased," I said as tears began to form.

"Have you tried to make friends with the students that are teasing you?"

"I tried, but it's no use."

"Have you ever tried to get involved in school activities?"

"No."

"Would you be interested?"

"I never thought about it."

"Maybe you should try something that is outside of your norm."

"Yeah, I think you might be right."

"Do you feel better now that we talked, Melanie?"

"Yes, I feel a lot better."

"Well, good, I want you know I'm always here for you."

"Thank you," I said, hugging Ms. Wright tight.

"You're welcome and take care, Melanie," she said, looking me in the eyes.

I decided to take the counselor's advice and try out for the school talent show. During the try outs, I sang a song from the Broadway play, Les Miserables titled "I

Dream a Dream."

As nervous as I was about singing in front of people, especially all those kids that teased me, it didn't help hearing them say, "She ain't gonna make it." I ignored them and stared at the chairs that were lined up in rows in the cold auditorium as if they were empty. I kept singing from my heart just like Shug told me to do.

When the audition was finally over, I felt like I had given my all in spite of the students laughing at me. The teacher wasn't very enthusiastic when she said, "Good job, Melanie, whoever is next please come up." To me that was a clear indication that I didn't make it. After the audition, I ran to the girls' bathroom and locked the door. I kicked the pink bathroom stall and covered my face with my hands. I listened carefully, holding back tears, to make sure there was nobody in the bathroom. The last thing I needed was more embarrassment. Once I knew that it was safe, I just began to sob. I had worked so hard on the song and practiced for hours, yet I still didn't even make the talent show.

✶✶✶✶✶

I was sitting in the cafeteria by myself with my journal

when I heard a girl speak, "Hello. I'm Ashley."
I looked up, surprised that someone had
acknowledged me and replied, "Hi, how are you?" I
flashed my amazing smile.
Luckily, Ashley hung with the popular crowd
sometimes, so I just knew I was in.
I would finally be able to be accepted by the upper
classmen and everyone else because Ashley is my
ticket in, I thought.
Boy was I wrong. Ashley introduced me to a girl
named Nish Lyles who was also a freshman and in our
classes. I didn't tell Ashley that I didn't want to meet
Nish because she talked about me all the time. If
Ashley had known that Nish talked about me, then
she probably would think I was a lame or something.
But she introduced us and smiled. I said hi to Nish
nonchalantly.
"Oh my God," Nish said. "I know you ain't friends
with her! Look at her. She's ugly and don't even know
how to dress."
"Nish, she is really nice! That's fucked up you would
say that about her to her face," Ashley responded.
Nish grinned. "Whatever...I call it like I see it and if
she is beat, then it is what it is and you shouldn't be

hanging with her."

Ashley left with Nish and told me she would see me later.

Looking obviously upset, I replied, "Yeah, whatever...we'll see." You could see that Ashley felt bad about what Nish had said about me, yet she still left with her.

My feelings were hurt. I sat back down at the table and continued writing in my journal. As I was writing a story, tears started to flow heavily down my cheeks. I wiped my face quickly in hopes that no one would see the tears. It was no use because I could feel them staring at me, but continued writing in the journal. I took a deep breath and said, "Mel...you are better than fine and you have no regrets." As I got myself together, I got up from the table to go sit in the courtyard, but before I got there the school bell rang, which meant lunch was over. I walked fast through the hallway, passing all the kids to get to my next class on time. When I made it to my class, I saw Ashley and Nish sitting next to each other.

"This is going to be a long class period," I whispered to myself.

The next few weeks seemed very long for me because I

was excited about the pep rally that was coming up.

"Two more days left until the pep rally," I said to my

friend Jewel while we were walking in the hallway.

"I know," Jewel said. "I am so excited! I can't wait!"

The day of the pep rally everyone was so hyped.

Students had face paint with the school mascot, a gray

cougar, painted on them with the year they would

graduate. The hallways were covered with the school

colors gray and navy blue. People were running up

and down the halls while the teachers were trying to

tell them to stop running, but of course no one

listened to them.

The day was dragging and the anticipation was

building. It was 12:50, and the freshman class of 2003

was lining up to go to the gym.

While I stood in line with Jewel, I could hear was "All

About the Benjamins" by Puff Daddy and Lil Kim

playing in the gym.

As the entire freshman class walked into the gym, they

took in all the decorations. There were blue and gray

cougar statues around the gym with art work and

posters made up by students from different classes.

The upperclassmen were all on the bleachers while

the freshman had to stand on the floor to watch the

show.

"Ain't this some shit. They get to be on the bleachers while we have to stand," I said folding my arms across my chest.

"Right doe, Mel! That is crazy," Jewel said, shooting a quick glance at the bleachers.

The show began with some of the seniors dancing to the Chris and Neef song "Can't Stop, Won't Stop." The seniors were doing all the latest dances and their own free styling. In the senior's group there were three boys and two girls. Everyone was enthusiastic and had great energy. The crowd went crazy. Their matching outfits were a nice touch. They wore white T-shirts with their name on them, and on the back of the shirt was their name with the year that they graduate spray painted in blue and gray.

Once the seniors were done, it was the junior class's turn to do their dance theme. Their group was just five boys. The juniors had on all black with their name on the front of their shirts and the year that they graduate on the back. Everybody thought that they were going to do a dance theme like the seniors, but instead they had a magic show prepared. They performed some really cool magic tricks. They pulled a bunny out of a hat, did a card trick with giant cards, and did a fire trick where someone lit a huge match and another person swallowed it. That was definitely the highlight of their performance and the enthusiastic crowd obviously agreed as they cheered and stood to their feet, except for the seniors.

I tried to clap extra loud to make up for the booing that came from the jealous seniors. Next it was the sophomores' turn. They were dressed in all black, too, but instead of having their names and class on the back, they had their own faces spray painted with the class on it. Their music choice was "Getting Jiggy Wit It" by Will Smith. When the song came on, three girls and four boys came out doing the "jiggy" dance. The teachers started laughing as they clapped their hands. One girl started doing the moonwalk in the audience and people were laughing and cheering her on. The sophomores had a soul train line going on while the music played.

While the pep rally was going on, a fight broke out in the crowd at the top of the bleachers.

"Awww shit, there is always a nucca spoiling the show for everyone, yanno, Jewel?" I noticed Jewel had left me and somehow got her tiny self up by where the fight was. The gym got so hyped and everyone was trying to get to the fight. I heard, "Whoop his ass, he don't even go here anyway, how the hell did he get in?"

A teacher got on the microphone and told everyone to settle down. Like they were gonna listen. But I was surprised that everyone got back to their seats. A cop came and escorted the students who broke into the pep rally out of the gym.

"That's what they get, they shouldn't be sneaking in here knowing this ain't even their school," I said to nobody in particular.

Once everyone was in their seats and were calm, the pep rally continued. All the freshmen that were posted on the floor started hollering and screaming so loud that people's voices started to crack. I screamed right along when the freshman crew came out on the dance floor. As I was screaming, my smile quickly disappeared because Nish was on the team. All I could think about was the terrible things Nish said about me. I turned to Jewel and said, "Should have known that she was going to be here."

All the freshmen were screaming when the song, "Oh No" by Noreaga came on. I just sat and looked with

my arms folded. I started to put my head down until
Jewel spoke, "Mel, have fun. So what she talks about
you. She's a stuck up bitch and everyone knows it."
I smiled at her and said, "You are so right. Fuck
Nish."

Nish was the only girl on the team. They wore white
T-shirt's with dark blue jeans and their shirts were
also spray painted with a cougar on it and on the back
it said, "Yea, we are freshmen, so what?" They danced
in a group to the song and the freshman class was
going crazy. They were hollering, stomping their feet,
throwing up signs from the hood that they
represented, and dancing.

"All this damn screaming is giving me a headache, oh
my God," I said, starting to lose my voice.

The freshmen were finally finished with their dancing
and then it was time for the homecoming King and
Queen to come out and give the nominees for the
future King and Queen. Once the nominees gave their
speech, everyone was escorted out to the bus to go
home.

When I got on the bus, I sat toward the front, praying
that the kids wouldn't tease me on the way home. As
soon as I got on the bus, someone yelled, "Dark Vader

is back on the bus again!" I let out a sigh of disgust then took my journal out of my backpack and wrote in it all the way until my stop came. It was just another day inside my crazy world.

*****

Everyone was talking about how good the pep rally was and how good homecoming was going to be. A couple of my friends asked me if I was going to homecoming.

"No," I replied. "With who? Nobody's gonna ask me." I had the biggest crush on this junior named Justin. We had study hall together and I would sometimes help him with his English papers. When we were in study hall, he was so nice and kind to me, but when he was around his boys it was a different story. His boys would joke and ask him, "Hey, Justin, you fuck with freshmen now?"

Justin would just casually respond, "Naw, I know her peoples."

It hurt my feelings that he lied to his friends, and he couldn't tell them that we were friends. Well, at least that's what I thought. I was in the library studying for

my math test when Justin walked in the library and
sat next to me.

I could feel myself getting excited between my legs
and I was really hoping it didn't show on my face. I
crossed my legs as tight as I could and took a deep
breath. I tried to think of some great thing to say but
what came out was:

"So, since you are like the star football player, I know
you are going to homecoming."

Justin, with a smirk on this face, said, "It's my duty to
go."

"Who are you taking, Nish?" I said hoping the answer
would be no.

All the guys loved Nish, and I could see why; she had
long pretty hair, was popular, dressed in nothing but
name brand, and had the body of a supermodel. She
always had a ride to school while me and everyone
else envied her 'cause we rode the school bus. You
knew you were somebody when you were a freshman
and didn't have to take the bus.

"I was thinking about it, but no I ain't taking her,"
Justin said. "I was thinking about taking you."

My heart felt like it dropped down to my stomach and
then went back to it's proper place. I must not have

been hearing things right? Seeing him smiling still, I asked "Really?"

"Sure, it's the least I can do since you have helped me in English."

I was happy he was even willing to show up with me that I didn't care why. With excitement apparent in my face, I quickly responded "Yes" and we exchanged numbers. From that moment on, happiness filled the air and no one could steal my joy.

On the way to chorus class, I was so excited about what had happened between me and Justin that I couldn't wait to tell Jewel the great news. As I walked into class, I was glad to see that there was a substitute teacher so I could spill the dirt. When Jewel heard the news, she said, "Oh my God! How the hell did you get him to ask you?"

"He just asked on his own."

"See, Melanie! You are a sweet person and people are starting to notice."

"I guess chivalry ain't dead after all," I said, giving Jewel a high five.

"I guess not and I am happy for you, Mel."

Homecoming was supposed to be one of the best days of your life besides your wedding, and I was ready for it.

Chapter 3

It was the day of homecoming and I had butterflies in my stomach. I had asked Justin what I should wear and he told me to wear black dress pants and a dress shirt. I thought people wore gowns and tuxes at a homecoming, but I was like, whatever, dress shirt and pants it is. I got an early dismissal that day from school to get my hair and nails done.

While waiting to be called to get shampooed, the door opened and the bell rang. It was Nish, my worst nightmare. She had on a white t-shirt with gray sweat pants and gray and white Air forces. She went to the front desk and gave her name to the receptionist. I just sat in the silver chair waiting impatiently to be called.

I kept saying to myself, "God I hope she doesn't see me." I repeated this to myself over and over again in my mind. Finally, my name was called, and I rose from my seat like it was on fire. I sat in the chair in the back of the salon and the stylist began to shampoo my hair. When I sat back in the chair under the sink, the stylist was smacking on her gum so loud, it was beginning to annoy me.

"What you getting your hair did for?"

"I'm going to homecoming dance at my school." I said, smiling hard.

"Oh that's nice. So then I have to make you look sharp, girl."

Once the shampooing was done, I went under the hair dryer and found myself sitting directly next to Nish. Luckily, my hair dried first and I had to sit in another chair to get my hair curled, away from Nish. I was happy because the quicker I got out of the salon, the better. I did find it odd that she didn't say anything to me.

After a half hour, my hair was finally finished. It was styled in a wrap and curled out. When the stylist gave me a mirror to look at my hair, everyone in the salon was telling me how good my hair looked. I blushed and said thank you, then walked out of the salon. For once in a long time, I felt beautiful.

Once I got home and got ready I sat downstairs, waiting for Justin to show up. Forty-five minutes went by and he didn't come; then all of a sudden there was a knock on the door and the butterflies returned to my stomach. Justin arrived at the door with a black and white corsage that matched my outfit. I had on a nice white blouse with buttons going down it and black dress pants. My nails were painted clear and I wore black high heels.

He had on a nice khaki tan shirt and black khaki pants. I felt kind of silly only because we didn't match. Shug stood with the camera and he said that there wasn't time and we had to get going. When we got in the car, he told me that I looked pretty. It felt so good when he said that because I worked extra hard on my appearance not only for him, but for the people that teased me in school. He even opened the door for me.

The silence in the car was deafening. Every so often I looked over at him. He was so cute, I just wanted to stop the car and tongue-kiss him right there on the road. I knew he could feel my eyes on him. He kept his eyes on the road, but did treat me to a few Hollywood-perfect smiles.

We pulled up to our school and he parked in the student parking lot. He again opened the car door for me and we walked hand and hand. I felt beyond special and was beaming with confidence. We got to the door and gave the teacher our tickets.

"Hey," Justin said abruptly, turning to face me, "I'll be right back. I need to use the bathroom. Go inside, and I'll be there soon."

"Okay," I said smiling.

As I walked in, I noticed the decorations in the gym; some with football decorations and different styles of musical notes, florescent colored lights all around and loud music playing. There was also a refreshment table in the back where teachers milled around. I guess they were supposed to be chaperoning everything but judging by the way everyone was dancing, they weren't doing a good job. Everyone was with their own crowd dancing and talking with their friends when I saw Justin and the football team in tuxedos. Then it dawned on me that all the girls had gowns on and all the men had tuxes on.

I walked up to Justin and asked him, "Why do you have on a tuxedo and when did you have time to change clothes?"

Before he could answer Nish walked up to me and said, "Wow, Justin! You really brought her? Give me my $50, boy! Don't even play...you know you owe me."

"What the fuck is she talking about?" I said with my hands on my hips.

"Now you didn't think he asked you because of your

good looks or the way you dressed. I mean come on!
Who comes to homecoming in dress pants?" Nish
said, throwing her hands up.

I couldn't take it anymore. My blood was boiling and I
shouted, "I am not talking to you at all!"

At that moment my heart was broken. Not only did I
think he liked me for me, but I also thought he was a
halfway decent guy. Nish was still saying things, but I
somehow blocked her out and went into one of the
empty classrooms and began writing on the
chalkboard. I didn't know what the hell I was writing,
but the more I wrote, the better I felt.

Justin found where I was and came into the
classroom. When he looked at me, tears were
streaming from my eyes like mini waterfalls. I had
never felt so stupid and ugly in my life.

Justin went to speak and I cut him off, "You know, it's
one thing to put me down and make yourself feel
good, but to humiliate me in front of the school is just
fucked up. God don't like ugly and he ain't to fond of
pretty."

Justin waited for me to take a breath and quickly said,
"Well, I'll take you home because the bet was just to
ask you, bring you, and have you dress different from

everyone else, and I did my part." He said without emotion.

When he said that, the tears started coming down even harder. There was makeup all over my white blouse.

"I will take that ride home only because I have no other way, you black bastard."

"Whatever. Just come on." He said walking towards the door.

In the car, I looked out the window and at the full moon. There were so many thoughts going through my head. I could feel the beginnings of a headache forming. We had been driving for like 15 minutes and weren't even in town yet.

"Where are we going 'cause we ain't nowhere near my house," I said.

He never answered me. Instead, he pulled up in the woods somewhere; it was dark as hell. He turned the car off and just sat there. Immediately, I felt uncomfortable and scared. He unbuckled his seatbelt and started kissing me on my neck.

"Take me home!" I said pulling away.

He then started unzipping his pants and pulling his boxers down.

"What the hell do you think you are gonna do with that? Keep that dick in your pants where it belongs." He told me to bend down and suck his dick. I looked at him like he had been smoking crack or something. Then he grabbed the back of my neck with force and said, "If you don't do it, I will push you out my car and leave you here bitch."

The tears started again. "I don't want to do it."

He squeezed my neck so hard that it started to pinch as he pulled my neck down to his crotch. The look in his eyes was pure evil.

I have no clue where I am, I thought. For all I know I'm in bumblefuck somewhere. I looked around to see if there were any gas stations or anything so I could get the hell out of there. There was nothing around, nothing but woods, trees, and darkness. I started to say a prayer, Lord, please forgive me for this sin that I am about to make and please make sure that I return home safely, but if something happens to me, I want you know that I was on this earth to serve you and I did my best. In Jesus' name I pray, amen.

I said the prayer over and over in my head. Then I finally did it.

I didn't know what I was doing at all, but he said if he

felt teeth that he would leave me out in the middle of nowhere. I was down there suffocating for at least ten minutes which felt like a lifetime.

All he kept saying was, "Suck it, Mel. That's right, suck it."

My stomach was in knots and I felt so nauseous. I had gotten so dizzy that I thought I would pass out. I figured I was finished performing the oral sex because all of a sudden I felt this warm liquid in my mouth which caused me to open the door and vomit.

Once I closed the door, he zipped his pants up, smiled at me and drove off from the dark place that I would never forget. As he started driving out of the woods, I started to see landmarks that looked familiar to me. It was quiet in the car except for me crying.

"What you crying for?" Justin asked. "You act liked I raped you." He said nonchalantly.

I looked at him and saw the devil in disguise. I couldn't believe he had the nerve to go there. "You did rape me! You held me against my will and took advantage of me!"

When we pulled up in front of my house, Justin said, "If you tell anyone what happened I will make your life a living hell."

I shook my head and said, "Before tonight I already thought it was hell, but tonight was just icing on the cake. I am officially living in it."

Justin opened the door and I slammed it and ran into the house. As I was running up the stairs, I could hear Shug yelling, "Did you have a good time?"

"Yea, I did." I felt so bad because I had never lied to my grandmother.

"You home awful early. You sure you had fun?" The truth was sitting on the tip of my tongue wanting to fly off. I wanted to tell her so badly what Justin had made me do, but I couldn't. All I kept hearing was, "I'm going to make your life a living hell." I ignored Shug and got in the shower. I stood in the shower feeling so dirty and unwanted. Eventually I lay in the shower in the fetal position as tears poured from my eyes. I even hit the bathtub a couple times. I tried not to cry too loud because I didn't want Shug to hear me.

When I got out of the shower, I began to get sick to my stomach again. I brushed my teeth and gargled with mouthwash constantly because that horrific moment kept playing in my head. Finally, I got up enough strength to get in bed, but couldn't sleep a wink. I couldn't stop worrying what people were going to say about me in school the next day.

Chapter 4

The next morning, my alarm clock went off, and I felt like I had just gone to sleep. After I hit the snooze button a few times, Shug came into my room and told me it was time to get up.

"Yes. Mum Mum, I know I have to get up, but I don't feel well." I said trying to sound as convincing as I could.

"Girl," Shug said, "you are getting out of here." She said pulling the covers off of me.

Okay, I thought, I'll get dressed and go to the bus stop and then let the bus leave me then say I missed the bus or it came early. Shug usually left when I walked to the bus stop.

I reluctantly got up, got dressed and left the house. The sun was barely out and the wind was sharp. As I walked toward the bus, I could barely keep my eyes open.

"I wish this bus would hurry up, so I can let it leave," I muttered.

About 15 minutes later, the bus came and I let it ride right by me. As it was leaving, I started to walk down the hill in order to get back to the house. Walking down the street, I passed the hustlers on the block selling their drugs; it pissed me off. Only because the same stuff they were selling, someone was giving it to my mother. One of them in a black pea coat pulled out some cocaine, and I watched him open it up and put some of it on his teeth.

Why in the hell would he do that in public and why would he put it on his teeth, I thought.

When I got back home, I saw Shug's car still parked.

"Ain't this about a bitch?"

Shug worked for the school district as a teacher, and her job was a long way from home. She usually left early to get there on time.

When I got inside the house, I climbed the stairs and walked in my room. I took off my Reeboks and lay on the red and yellow rose comforter.

I wasn't asleep a good half hour when Jackie came in the room and asked, "Why you still here?" while snacking on some cereal.

She stood there in one of my grandmother's purple housecoats with her hair all over her head looking crazy.

"Mom," Jackie hollered, "Melanie came back in and laying in the bed."

"Oh my God," I said, "you are such a snitch, always telling something. Go back out and get high."

My mom smacked me in the face. "You don't give a damn what I do! I am your mother and you are going to respect me." I just rolled my eyes.

"Why are you here?" Shug asked as she came through the door.

"I missed the bus, Mum Mum."

"Okay. Let me put something on so I can take you to school."

I sucked my teeth and rolled my eyes. When Shug made her mind up, that was it. There was no changing it.

We got in the car and started to pull off and I began to cry.

"What's wrong?" Shug asked. "Why are you crying?"

I lied and told her I didn't feel good. Then, I thought about telling her the truth. However, I quickly changed my mind when I had a flashback of Justin saying, "If you tell I will make your life a living hell."

We pulled up in front of the school and I got out the car. I entered and was walking in the hallway about to go to English class when I saw that everyone was whispering, laughing, and pointing at me. I started to

feel uneasy and wondered if Justin had told everyone
what happened on homecoming night.

In English class I was reading a book because I
finished my paper early. I was getting lost in the book
when Nish said, loud enough so that everyone could
hear, "I told Justin you were easy and that he could
fuck you and you would suck his dick."

I sat there with my book in my hand and then I looked
at the teacher who of course wasn't paying attention
to the class at all.

"Bitch, whatever," I said. "Ain't anything easy about
me and Justin didn't do shit to me."

"Well that ain't what he telling everyone else, slut."

I slammed the book down in rage. "I got your slut!"
The teacher finally noticed that something was going
on, and said, "Okay, class, settle down." I was so
pissed at this point, wanting to punch Nish right in
her damn face.

I excused myself from the class and went to the
bathroom. In the stall there was my name and phone
number written in permanent black marker, "Will
fuck if you act interested in her because she is easy."
The English Teacher, Mrs. Dunn, came into the
bathroom to check on me and I pointed to the stall

with my name and phone number along with the note.
"Oh my God, Melanie," Mrs. Dunn said. "Are you
alright, sweetheart? Honey, everything is going to be
okay. Do you know who did this?"

"Nish," I gritted out through clenched teeth.

Once I got myself together, I went back to class.

"Damn, girl," Nish said. "You took long in the
bathroom! Were you fucking or sucking somebody off
in there?" Everyone in the class laughed again.

"Yea, your mom taught me all I needed to know, so
when you get home tonight don't forget to ask her
who your real daddy is."

Nish jumped up like she was ready to fight, and I
stood there waiting for her to swing, praying for her to
hit me. All of a sudden, Mrs. Dunn stepped in and
told Nish to go to the principal's office. I left the
classroom and went to the Wellness Center.

The Wellness Center was a clinic in the school where
they had STD testing and counseling with specialists
you talked to about sex. I had always gone to the
wellness center to talk to Ms. Keer when I was having
problems or needed someone to listen. I was there
often, and it always gave me an excuse to miss class.

I explained to Ms. Kerr what happened, and she urged

me to tell someone else besides her. I didn't but I felt a
little better because at least someone else knew.

By the time I was finished speaking with Ms. Kerr it
was lunchtime. Ashley wanted to sit with me, not as a
friend but to know if the rumors that were being
spread about me were true. I never gave her an
answer and she just left the table. Jewel saw me and
asked if I was okay. I could trust Jewel because she
was just about the only true friend I had in school.
Everyone else was shady. They were cool with me
when they thought it was convenient for them which
was usually if we had a group project to do.

As Jewel and I were laughing about chorus class, we
saw Justin and he was with Nish. I looked their way
and rolled my eyes at both of them.

The next couple of days there were all these boys
talking about how they liked me and I was so pretty. I
knew that it was all game because my phone number
kept popping up in the girls' bathroom and the
teacher had told me that it was removed.

I hate this damn school, I thought. I can't wait until it
is over so I can transfer somewhere else.

This boy named Jeff came up to me in study hall and

spoke sympathetically, "I'm sorry to hear what people are saying about you, but I know that ain't true. You don't seem like that type of girl at all."

I didn't know whether to say thank you or leave me the fuck alone.

"I'm not like all the other guys here at school. I may be a senior, but I respect women." Jeff smiled at me and I gave him a slight grin. He gave me a hug and as he hugged me I just started crying. He hugged me harder and whispered, "It's okay. I'm here for you if you ever need to talk." Quickly I got off him and apologized. He just said, "It's cool. I can tell you needed to hear that."

I looked at him hard, wondering if he were a bullshitter or a nice guy.

I gave him another grin and then walked towards the door and told him I would see him around.

"You sure will." Then he yelled, "Wait. Your poem that you had in the school paper. I really liked it."

I left smiling at him with my cheeks a little flushed. I thought that was so nice, but my guard was still up just in case he was another Justin.

Although it didn't feel like he was.

I had to hurry to get to the auto body shop class even

though I hated it. Learning about cars was something that I didn't see a career in. At Pointe High, you had to go to every shop that was offered and when you got to the tenth grade, you could pick the shop you wanted.

Auto body was the last shop and then school was out, thank God. I wanted to leave Pointe High as soon as I got there. The only reason I attended the school was because both my brothers Terron and Q went.

I ended up being late to auto body class and the teacher, Mr. Melvin, asked if I was okay. I just responded "Yeah" and left it at that. Nish also was in class, so there was never a break.

"I'm so glad that I don't have to wear weave unlike some bald headed people," Nish said snickering.

I just closed my eyes and ignored her. I sat in the front row of the class so I could pay more attention to the lesson. Once the teacher finished taking roll, he said that the class had to observe the horn of this old truck to show that it wasn't working correctly for our assignment.

"Everyone, look at the front of the truck," Steven said.

"Okay, we're looking, and...?" A girl said uninterested.

"If you look, I am pressing on the horn and it's not

working."

"Oh okay I see now," the same girl said sarcastically.
We stood to the side in a single file line out of the way
of the demonstration. Everyone else backed up and
was done looking, but I was still looking. Steven got in
the truck and started it up. I was standing in front of
the truck and wasn't paying attention. Next thing I
knew I heard, "Oh shit, Melanie, watch out." The truck
had skidded and there I was on the ground.

All I could hear was laughing from the whole class.
Pain rushed throughout my legs.

"That's exactly what she get," I heard someone yell.

"Oh my God. Are you okay, Melanie?" the teacher
asked rushing over to me.

The class continued laughing.

"It's not funny," I yelled on the brink of tears.

Mr. Melvin helped me to my feet and to the door. I
limped out of class and down the narrow hallway to
the nurse's office. I held on to the wall the whole way
there. Ms. Wright's smile faded when I entered the
room.

"What's wrong, sweetie?"

"A boy hit me with a truck in the auto body class."

"Oh my God. Are you okay?"

"If I were okay, I would not be here, Ms. Wright." I
said annoyed.

"Tell me where it hurts."

"My thighs."

"Let's go into the back room so I can have a look at
them. We don't want the entire nurse's office to see
you."

"Okay."

"It hurts for me to try to get my jeans off," I said
trying to get them off.

"I know, sweetheart, but I have to see," she said,
feeling on my thigh which had began to swell.

"I am going to pull your emergency card and
get your parents' number so you can go to the
hospital."

"It hurts so bad."

"I know it does, sweetie, now get dressed and come sit
in the waiting area while I call your parents."

About 30 minutes later, Shug stormed in the nurse's
office looking ready for war.

"Why didn't y'all call the ambulance and report what
had happened?" she yelled at the nurse. I could hear
her yelling at the principal who had now entered the
office.

"No motherfucker! You were supposed to notify me as soon as it happened. I'm suing the shit out this damn school and you don't even have to worry about her coming back next year!"

When I did arrive back at school, it was the last day. I couldn't believe that Shug sent me to school on the last day. Who does something like that? The funny thing is that Shug ended up suing the school because of my leg bruise.

When I got off the bus, everyone was staring and laughing at me.

"Did you get hit by a truck?" someone asked, laughing. I just ignored them and thought, This is my last day here, so I ain't even worrying about it. I got to my classes so late that day because it was hard for me to get around from the accident. On top of that, the prescription pills weren't helping.

I was a little excited that day because report cards came out and I wanted to know how I did. I was sitting in homeroom when Mrs. Dunn handed my report card to me. I stared at it for a minute because I couldn't believe my eyes. I had made honor roll again with straight A's!

"Wow Mel, you did good," I said to myself.

Through Her Eyes

I had gotten honor roll that whole year and didn't
understand how, but I just thanked God. I was so
proud of myself. The day was a blur, and by the end
of it, I was so relieved that the nightmare that lasted
for a year was now finally over.

Chapter 5

Finally, a new year and a new school. It was a little more comfortable for me at City High because I knew almost everyone. The people I knew at City High went to the same middle school as I did. As soon as I walked in the school to go to my first period class, I was greeted by some of my old friends. It felt great to me not to be teased.

Lunch time that day was a little different than Pointe High. Everyone had lunch mostly at the same time. The lunch room was buzzing with activity. I could barely hear myself think with all the loud conversations going on. I navigated through the thick crowd and found a table. While I was sitting there, a guy who had to be every bit 6'3, sat next to me and said, "You know, this is only where seniors sit."

I looked at him like, Wow he is really tall, then I said to him, "Oh, ok. I'll move." I quickly got up from the table and sat with my cousin Dee.

"Dee, what's up?" I said getting comfortable at the lunch table.

"Hey Mel, ain't nothing up, girl. I'm pissed I had to come to school though."

"Yea, and thanks for telling me that the seniors had their own place to sit." I said slapping her playfully across the forearm.

"You're welcome," she said, smiling. "Girl, you ain't changed a bit. What class do you have next?"

"I have gym next and I can't stand it."

"Yea, I hear you, girl. I got Spanish, but all I do is sleep in there."

"Girl, you better stay up and learn that espanol!"

"Yea ok," Dee said, rolling her eyes. "I'll see you later."

"Bye!"

✴✴✴✴✴

Once I got to gym, I walked to the girls' locker room to change in those crazy blue and gold uniforms. The gym teacher, Mr. Yelp, told us to get into our squads. Once he took roll, he made us run around the gym three times straight. I was not feeling that at all. I was standing in line waiting for my turn when I heard, "Yea, she aight. I mean she ain't no dime or nothing, but I would fuck her only because she got big titties." I turned around and looked at the guy that said it. He looked puzzled because he didn't think I heard him. "Sorry, I don't fuck with light brights. Their dicks look too much like white boys, and they usually small anyway." I said holding my pointer finger and my thumb close together, indicating the size.

"Oh shit, yo," the boy's friend yelled. "She punked the shit out of you!"

The boy stared at me, silent.

As I ran my laps, I felt eyes on me and of course they were his. I wasn't stupid. I knew he was looking at my breasts while I was running. After everyone ran their laps, gym was over and I couldn't be more thrilled.

Now it was off to chorus class. Chorus class was always fun because not only did I know everybody, but the teacher was one of my third grade teachers. I was trying out for chorus, and Mrs. Sare told me that I had a beautiful voice, so she put me in the soprano section.

Once everyone was placed in a section, we started working on a new song right away. I was excited because there was a concert coming up and I wanted my family there to see me because I was trying out for the solo.

That day I got home and told Jackie and Shug about my day at school. I was happy Jackie was awake this time and she seemed interested in what I had to say.

Through Her Eyes

With her crack and cocaine candy, my mother was hardly there to talk to or be supportive. I always wished Jackie would get tired and stop using one day. I knew it wouldn't happen overnight but I had faith that it would happen sooner than later.

Chapter 6

During my Junior year I made friends with all the administrators in the school as well as the nurses. I also ended up trying out for cheerleading. The senior cheerleaders laughed at me despite my efforts, "Why did you even waste your time on trying out? You ain't gon' make it." they said.

I tried out because I wanted to try something new and the uniforms were so cute. Trying new things that I normally wouldn't do was exciting to me. I wanted to quit as soon as the girl said that smart comment, but then I thought, If I quit, I will never know if I had a chance at making it. So I kept going with the routine. I tried my hardest and followed the dance moves to a T. To my surprise I didn't make the team. After my attempt at cheerleading I tried out for drama class. I was trying to hype myself up. I didn't want to deal with the letdown if I didn't succeed at the drama thing. After I tried out, the teacher politely told me that I didn't have any acting skills. It felt like a slap in the face but I had to keep it moving.

On a positive note, the school made a talent book in which they published students' art, stories, poetry,

and other artistic endeavors. I had five poems
published in the book, and when they were published,
everyone was telling me how talented I was. The
principal, Dr. Lawyer, wanted to see me in his office.
What did I do? I thought, scared. I never get in
trouble.

He had the talent book in his hand when I walked in.
Leaning back in his black leather chair gazing at the
book, he looked up at me and said, "Miss Woodard,
I'm sorry to interrupt you from class, but these poems
here are extraordinary."

"Thank you, Dr. Lawyer," I said, smiling.

"You have a gift for writing and I was wondering why
you're not writing in the journalism club."

"I didn't apply although I did write a sample piece. I
decided not to join 'cause I have a job now and I won't
be fully committed to the club."

"I can understand that," Dr. Lawyer said, "but I can't
wait until you write a book. You are an exceptional
writer."

It felt good to hear him say that about my writing.
Maybe I would be a great writer someday. I was
inspired by my boyfriend at the time, Ben, to start
writing. I had written him a poem one day in my study

hall, and I entered it into a contest and won five hundred dollars. That's when I knew that I was good at writing. We had been dating for about two months now and I was so in love.

Ben was twenty three and I was seventeen at the time. Ben and I met one day while I was walking to Family Dollar. I thought he was cute the minute I saw him. Ben had asked me how old I was and I told him the truth. Sometimes I would lie about my age to guys. The first time I invited him over to my house, I was nervous. I put my key in the door and of course as soon as I opened the door, everyone was all downstairs like they were waiting for us. My hands shook badly as Ben and I went to the couch and sat down. I groaned; my uncle lay on the couch all the time, so much so that now it felt like his body was imprinted on the couch.

My house was a little dirty and I was so embarrassed. Not only embarrassed at the house, but embarrassed that Ben was there and I didn't know if he would judge me based on how my house looked. There was paper everywhere and roaches were climbing on the walls. The house was always a mess and as much as I would clean it, my uncles made it dirty it again. That

was one of the many reasons I hated living with Shug.
Terron was the first to grill Ben.

"So, Ben," he said, "do you have a job?"

Ben opened his mouth, and Terron yelled, "No!"

"Yes," Ben replied nicely, "I do. I work construction."

All the men said in unison, "He ain't got no damn job!"

Shug, God bless her, welcomed him, but I could tell she had her horns sticking up, too.

Jackie just came out and asked, "You fucking my daughter?"

"Oh my God, Mom," I screamed, humiliated. "I can't believe you just asked that."

Everybody eyed us, and in unison, Ben and I replied, "No."

"Sweetie," Shug said, looking at Ben, "how old are you?"

"He's twenty-three, Mum Mum," I answered for him.

"What does a twenty-three-year-old want with a girl who just turned seventeen?" Terron asked. "Ben, I'm going to tell you right now. You are slick and you're so slick when you walk past me I can see oil puddles. I feel it in my spirit something ain't right about him."

Everyone else except Shug agreed. I was pissed, and

Ben had this crazy look on his face.

"I'll call you later," Ben said before getting up to leave the house.

When he left, I yelled, "Y'all are so embarrassing!"

I stormed upstairs and closed my bedroom door. I flopped on the bed, turned on the radio, and stewed; I was so mad I couldn't even remember going to sleep.

When I woke up, I quickly grabbed my phone to see if Ben had called me and he didn't.

"Damn," I muttered, "the boy don't even want to talk to me anymore."

I was so upset at how my family treated Ben. It wasn't until two days later Ben had called me and said that he still wanted to date me. I can still remember when my phone rang.

"Hello."

"Hey, Mel."

"Ben?"

"Yea, it's Ben who else is it supposed to be? Your not seeing anyone else are you?" he said letting out a laugh.

"Honestly I didn't know if I was seeing you by the way my family reacted when I brought you home."

"Nah I wasn't worried about that, family will be family right?"

"You can say that again."

"So, what's up, Mel, you want to go to a movie or something?"

"Sure, I would love that."

"Okay be ready in an hour."

"Alright Sweety, see you later."

"Alright, Sexy, goodbye."

"Bye."

Hanging up the phone, I was so excited and ready for our date. I was so relieved that Ben still wanted to be with me.

Senior prom was right around the corner. Everyone was asking if I was going, but I said no only because I couldn't take Ben because of the age restriction. I was excited because it was the day for me to take my senior pics. We had to take our senior pics in our junior year.

"Mom, my pics are being done today, and my hair looks a mess."

"Mel, just gel it into a ponytail. You got enough hair, don't you?"

She started laughing after she said that.

"Ha ha, Mom, you got jokes today I see."

"Okay let me see, I know a crack head who does good hair." She said in a tone like it was an everyday thing for a crack head to do your hair.

"Mom, I'm serious and stop calling people crack heads when you do the same thing."

"Melanie, I'm not a crack head. I just get high from time to time."

We both couldn't help but laugh after she said that. She was crazy.

"Mel, do you want me to call her or what, it's your pictures." She said like she was getting annoyed.

"Okay, Mom, call her but if she has me looking crazy, I'm blaming you."

I couldn't believe she actually called a crack head to do my hair. After about 15 minutes Kira showed up at the door. She went through her bag while I sat in the chair. I closed my eyes and prayed that she knew what she was doing.

"Keep your fuckin' head still, girl, damn," Kira said.

"Just 'cause you know me from the streets, bitch, don't mean we that cool," Jackie said. "Don't talk to mine's that way."

"I'm sorry, Jackie."

"Just hurry up with my daughter's head so you can have this five dollars to go get you a hit. You trippin' talkin' to my daughter like you crazy. I don't play when it comes to my children, high or not high. You need to know that."

Wow, I couldn't believe Jackie was sticking up for me like that. I guess she really did love me. I used to question her love for me only because she was using. I always thought if she would hurt me by using then she only cared for herself. I always felt me and my brother were on the back burner.

Maybe we weren't.

*****

"Daddy, what if I smile wrong, or not look at the camera man."

"Melanie, you have a beautiful smile, you will do fine," he said, boosting my confidence a little.

"Okay, but you always say that."

"That's because it's always true. And who did your hair, it looks nice."

Trying to hold in my laugh, I said, "Dad, you wouldn't believe me if I told you, but thanks for the compliment."

"Melanie Woodard, you're up next."
I walked up and sat in the chair to get the casual picture done first.
As I took shot after shot, I smiled. I felt so happy and excited that I was going to be a senior next year and I would finally be graduating high school.

Chapter 7

It was now senior year at City High. I was graduating in May and was proud of it. I was still in chorus and had become a nurse's aide. I loved being in the nurse's office because I was able to see all the kids who would come play sick just to go home. A freshman came in and said, "I don't feel good, I think I have prostate cancer." I laughed so hard that I almost peed my pants. I mean who says that? The nurses had to laugh, too. They gave the boy a pass to go right back to class.

"So Melanie, now that you are a senior, what are your plans for college?" the lead nurse Mrs. Reid said.

"Well I want to go, but I don't have the money to be able to." I said as my mood saddened a little.

"Have you applied anywhere?"

"Yea, Del-State University, Wilmington College, University of Delaware, and Delaware Tech."

"Wow, that's a lot of schools."

"I really want to go to Del-State."

"I hope you get in."

"Thank you, Mrs. Reid."

The next day while I was sitting in homeroom my

friend Will asked me if I was going to prom. I told him that I was and that I'd probably go alone.

"Well, I don't have a date either, so why don't we just go to together?"

"Cool. It's a date," I said, smiling.

Will was always nice to me, but the popular boys always teased him for some reason and I could never understand why. Will was nice, cute, and smart, but he only spoke when he was spoken to, and I knew about that more than anybody.

Shug ended up taking me to David's Bridal, and I found the perfect gown for prom. It was rose and silver with silver embroidery going down the sides and it flared out at the bottom. The shoes were clear slippers like Cinderella and boy did I feel like Cinderella. When I put on my gown, Shug started crying because she said I looked so beautiful. I was always a sensitive person so when Shug started crying, it made me cry, too.

"Mum Mum, stop it. You're making me cry."

"I'm sorry, Melanie, it's just that I raised you and now you are all grown up, going to prom."

"You did a great job raising me, too."

"Thank you, baby," she said, wiping her tears.

"Well if this Will doesn't like you now, he will after he
sees you in this dress."

"Mum Mum, you a mess."

On prom night, Shug helped me get dressed. Jackie
was there to help me get dressed, too. I treasured the
bond that we were forming. My dad wasn't able to
make it to the house to take pictures, but he bought
me a corsage which was beautiful. It had white roses
dipped in silver with a hint of rose in it.   Q took me to
the mall to get my makeup done.

"Q, this makeup is itching me."

"Melanie, you never wore make up before?" he
quizzed.

"No."

"Are you serious? Wow."

"Don't wow me, Q, every time I wanted to wear it, you
told me I was too young for it."

"You still are too young now, but prom is special." He
said smiling.

"I'm eighteen now. I'm not a child anymore!"

"You are what I say you are."

"Q, do me a favor and grow up."

"You want me to grow up like you, Ms. Itching

Makeup?"

After we got back, I got dressed and was ready to go. As I began to walk downstairs, I started to get butterflies in my stomach. I didn't want a repeat of my past experiences.

I wanted to know who the prom king and queen were going to be, what color dress Dee was going to wear; I wanted to see and know everything.

When I got outside, everyone was out there including Jackie, my cousin Toy, my cousin Bingo, and her twin cousins Eryc and Erycka. They were waiting for Will to come so they could take pictures and be on their way. Just when I started to get aggravated, Will arrived in a gorgeous black Benz.

"Aw shit," I said to myself.

Will stepped out looking like a different person. He looked good in his black tux. He had his hair cut low and dyed black. He cleaned up real nice. Everyone was snapping pictures. I felt like I was a famous singer and they were paparazzi.

Will opened the door for me and I stepped in. He closed my door and got into the driver's seat. We pulled off and I could see my family still watching as the car pulled off.

Will and I got to prom and as we walked in, everyone
stopped and ran up to us, telling us how good we
looked. I looked around and some girls had on halter
top gowns that looked ridiculous.

When I saw Dee, I smiled. She looked so pretty. She
had on a sky blue gown that hugged her slender body
and her shapely booty. Her dress flared out at the
bottom. Her hair was in a pretty bun that was cocked
to the side. She had on flawless makeup that made
her skin glow perfectly. I began to tear up.

"Bitch," she said, "your sensitive ass always crying."

I really enjoyed myself that night. I danced, took
pictures, ate, and then went home. There was an after
party, but I didn't go because I wanted to be with Ben.
Ben didn't call me or show up that night after prom.
Pissed off was an understatement.

The next morning I woke up and found three
voicemail messages on my phone. I knew that they
were from Ben. I called my voicemail and listened to
the messages.

Message one: "Mel, I'm sorry that I didn't show up,
baby. I was with my boy and got caught up in some
shit. I love you. Call me back."

Message two: "Mel, I know you probably still sleep,

but I hope you ain't too mad at me, baby. It's not my fault. I tried to get there. Okay, call me back."

Message three: "Mel, call when you wake up. Okay bye, I love you."

I deleted the three messages then went to my speed dial and called Ben. He answered on the third ring, "Hey baby."

"Don't fucking baby me. Why didn't you come to my crib?"

"Baby, I'm sorry. I got caught up in some shit with my boy, and I couldn't get to your house."

"Well, why didn't you call me?"

"My cell phone had died."

"Nucca, you know you lying 'cause if your phone was dead how did you call me three times in the middle of the night?"

There was silence on Ben's end.

"Ben, take that check to the bank and cash it somewhere else."

"Mel, that's the truth."

"Whateva, nucca. I gotta go."

"Wait." It was too late for him to finish his sentence. I had already hung up on his ass. I was so pissed that I threw my phone and broke it.

✳✳✳✳✳

Graduation day finally arrived and I was more than ready. At the rehearsal, it was so crowded in the school auditorium that it took the students an hour before we finally lined up correctly. We had to be paired up with partners to enter the B Center.

The newspaper did a nice write up about me weighing one pound at birth. They ran the article in the paper on graduation day. Ben called me that morning and congratulated me on graduating. Even though he was a knucklehead sometimes, I knew he had good intentions.

Everyone was talking about how much they were going to miss each other and I really began to appreciate my time there. Our alma mater's song started playing from the speakers and that was our cue to start walking. As soon as I walked out, I saw my aunts Levette and Debbie, Q, my dad and his new girlfriend, Pammy. I still couldn't believe he had divorced Ms. Sugar. On the other side, I saw Jackie, Shug, and my great grandma Margret. There were three generations standing before me.

I was in line and the next to be called. My heart was pounding and my hands were trembling.

When I was called, I walked up to shake the principal's hand and gave him the biggest hug ever. For the few seconds of glory, everyone was cheering for me and I was so excited; then they called the next person. That was the most accomplished feeling I had ever felt and I couldn't wait to start college in the fall. Once all the graduates' names were called, the class valedictorian gave a long speech about future endeavors.

"Oh my God," one of my classmates, Andrea said. "Does this speech have to be this damn long?"

 "I'm ready to get my diploma and leave already," I said.

"I know what you mean, Melanie."

Another ten minutes went by then we heard, "Class of 2003, congratulations!"

"That was like music to my ears," I said, "'cause another minute and I would have been sleep."

"Who you telling? I was already nodding off."

 We both started laughing and we gave each other a hug.

Once I greeted my family, we got in the car and left to go home. The feeling of having my diploma was more than I could imagine. I was looking forward to the next phase of my life.

Ben and I had been dating on and off for two years
now. Our relationship had seen its ups and downs. I
saw potential in him which is why I couldn't shake
him. For every negative thing he did he would quickly
make for it. I could admit that he was very charming
and that alone made me tingly inside. During the first
couple of months with Ben, he wouldn't try anything
on me. Then we went through a period where we
weren't even having sex at all. The moment we started
back up I had gotten on birth control. I didn't want to
chance anything.

Things had been going relatively alright until the week
I started going to community college. That week it was
almost like he picked a new thing to argue about. The
worst argument was yet to come. I had been upstairs
cleaning up when I heard the door. I looked out the
window and saw Ben standing at the door shifting his
weight from one foot to the other. There was no
mistaking the expression on his face. He was pissed
off and now I wanted to know why. I rushed
downstairs when the knocking intensified.

"I'm coming!" I yelled while I was halfway down the
stairs.

Soon as I unlocked the door, Ben stormed by me without saying anything. I followed him up the steps wondering what the hell had gotten into him. He was sitting on my bed with his hands clasped together looking at the ground. He lifted his head with the same expression on his face.

"Melanie, give me a hundred dollars." He said out the clear blue.

"Give you who?"

"I know you got it, come on, Mel."

"Last time I checked you were a grown ass man, older than me as a matter of fact."

"Baby, are you going to give it to me?"

"No, 'cause you don't know how to pay nobody back."

"What, I bought you clothes and shoes."

"Uh yes you did, but I didn't give you clothes and shoes to borrow, now did I?"

"Are you gonna give it to me?" he repeated.

"For the last time, Ben, no."

"You ain't gotta give it to me. I'll get it from the other girl I fuck with."

I couldn't believe what just came out of Ben's mouth.

"What? Well you do that then. I'll be alright," I said trying my best to hide the hurt.

I played if off on the outside but on the inside my heart was shattered into a million pieces. I had never cheated on Ben.

"You're ugly anyway," Ben said. "You need to fix this dirty house and get some new glasses."

How could he be so cruel and heartless? "This house wasn't all that dirty when you was fucking me in it, now was it? I don't know why all of sudden I need glasses when you bought these ones, you clown."

The tears started rolling down my cheeks as he was getting his clothes together. While he was packing, he was mumbling, "I can't believe I wasted two years for this bullshit."

"I don't give a damn what you say, just pack your shit and bounce."

"Melanie, leave me the fuck alone, man," he said as his voice got louder.

"I don't give a damn about you raising your voice. If that's what you have to do to feel like a man, then yell."

"Trust and believe me, you will need me before I need you."

He got quiet then all of a sudden, he stopped packing and sat on my bed. "Mel, my lights about to get cut off."

"Okay, Ben, then you need to return those two hundred dollars shoes and that hundred dollar outfit you just bought."

"Whatever, Melanie."

"Hey, Ben those are your lights. You gotta get your priorities straight or better yet ask that other girl you fucking, and since I'm ugly with a dirty house I can flick my lights on and off, can you?"

"Fuck you, Melanie." He said with his voice dripping with anger.

"See you. Get out of my dirty house."

"But I love you," he said with the most sincerity in his eyes, but I knew he was just trying me to see if I would give in and give him the money.

"Good bye, Ben." I said with finality.

He tried to kiss me, but I backed away. He grabbed the rest of his things and left the house. After Ben left, I went into Shug's room to vent. I walked in her room and lay on her bed while she was watching General Hospital. I didn't even say a word before she said, "Go ahead, Melanie, tell me what happened while the commercial is on."

"Mum Mum, it's Ben."

"I know that he said and did some things he probably didn't mean," she said, directing her full attention to me. "You were good to him," Shug told me. "He'll be back."

"I ain't taking him back." I said folding my arms across my chest.

"Sure you will. You are a woman scorned."

"I don't think so."

"Melanie, I have been there and back. Trust me I know."

Little did Shug know I was done with Ben completely.

Chapter 8

The next few months were better, now that I was over Ben. After that stunt he pulled, I decided that I was done with him and his bullshit. It was time to move on. There was this nice guy that I was talking to and it was time to really get to know him.

It was almost pitch black outside while I was waiting for Lay to come over my aunt's house. I waited in the freezing cold because the anticipation was killing me. After a few minutes, he pulled into the middle of the block. Lay got out of his black Grand Pre with a cool swagger about him.

He walked up to me and said smoothly, "Hi, Miss Lady. How you doing?"

"I'm doing fine," I said, nervously looking at the ground.

Lay was 5'9, caramel, with nice brown eyes that you could gaze into for decades and lips that were made for kissing.

Wow, I thought. He is so smooth.

He also smelled really good. He was dressed nicely from what I could see. He was wearing a black butter leather jacket with blue jeans and spotless white sneakers. We were just standing there in the cold looking at each other when he flashed his smile and said, "Are you going to invite me in?"

"Yes, I'm sorry. Where are my manners?"

My aunt's place was on the third floor, so we had to go up all those steps which I hated.

While we were hiking the stairs, my mind wandered: Does he like me, or is he just going to pretend he does and not call me again?

When we walked into the apartment, I told him that he could have a seat and make himself comfortable.

He took his jacket off and turned on the Eagles game. I hated football, but I would pretend to like it for him.

He looked at me with those deep brown eyes and asked, "So, sweetie, how was your day?"

"It was fine."

I knew he could feel my nervousness when he grabbed my hand and told me it was okay. He pulled me close as I sat on the couch.

When the game was on commercial, I grabbed the remote and put music videos on. Mario was playing and I loved me some Mario. We watched videos for a while when all of a sudden we heard the door open and close.

My aunt Becky's girlfriend barged in the house and shouted, "Where is Becky?"

I uneasily replied, "She went to do laundry and get me something to eat."

"Really. And she just left you in charge of the house, huh?"

I didn't say a word. I was so embarrassed because Lay just sat there holding back laughter.

My aunt Becky walked through the door and then both of them started arguing. I whispered to Lay, "I am so sorry that you have to be here for all of this."

"It's cool," he said, laughing it off.

My aunt Becky had an open cast on her foot from an accident that occurred at work so she was just limping and arguing. Her girlfriend started going down the steps to leave and they were still arguing on the way down. By this point, I was fully embarrassed.

He's not going to talk to me for sure now with all this drama, I thought. So much for our first time seeing each other.

My aunt Becky came back upstairs with a knot on her head. I just looked at her and shook my head.

Then I introduced her to Lay.

"Lay, I'm sorry that you are here to see this shit. I told

that bitch it was over. I don't know why she keep
coming here."

Lay and I started laughing immediately.

"It's aight." He said putting his hands in his pockets.

"Melanie, is this your man?"

"Aunt Becky!"

Lay started smiling sexily at me.

"We just friends right now," Lay replied, "but you
never know. I really like her."

I started blushing so hard that I was probably red in
the face. Then Lay said, "It was nice meeting you,
Becky, but I have to get going."

Lay asked me if I wanted a ride home and I happily
accepted. He helped put on my coat and my aunt
whispered, "Girl, he is a cutie." I just smiled at her.
We got in the car and there was this awkward silence,
something I had expected after what happened.

"I just wanted you to know I enjoyed myself, Mel, in
spite of everything." He put on his seatbelt.

"Yea, me too except for when my aunt's girlfriend
started arguing with her." Then all of a sudden, we
both burst out laughing. When we pulled up to my
house, I had those butterflies in my stomach again.
As I was unbuckling my seat belt, he softly grabbed

me and kissed me nice and slow. I never had a guy kiss me like that and as we kissed I felt this warm sensation surge throughout my body.

This is the one, I thought.

We said our goodnights and he waited until I got inside my house before pulling off. I thought it was so sweet for him to make sure I got in okay. I floated into the house and upstairs.

An hour later, my phone rang and I jumped up so fast to answer the phone, hoping Lay was the voice on the other end.

"Hello," I said, trying not to sound too eager.

Just as I was hoping, that sexy voice was on the other end. He said knowingly, "You didn't think I was going to call, did you?"

"To be honest? Nope. I didn't think you liked me."

"Melanie, if I didn't like you I would not have stayed as long as I did."

From that point on, Lay and I were inseparable. My family loved him, especially Shug. She said he was so nice and charming. Shug loved to hear Lay sing. He had met my family, but the only person I met in his family was his brother. I thought that was odd but of course paid no attention to it. He never talked about his mother that much at all either.

When I called Lay's house for him one day, his mother told me, "Lay is married." I didn't know what to think now. When I asked Lay about it, he would tell me that his mom didn't know what she was talking about. I ignored it for a while. But his mother never stopped telling me that he was married.

Despite that I felt like we were growing a lot in our relationship and we agreed to take it to the next level. I told my family we were engaged and they were thrilled. Lay and I set a date and everything. Shug loved Lay so much that he was even allowed to stay the night at the house.

Me, my friend Alexis, Jackie and Shug went shopping for my wedding dress. We went to David's Bridal and I was in heaven. They had all types of gowns in there; some lace, silk, traditional, and even more modern gowns. I told Jackie and Shug that I wanted to try on all of them.

"I didn't think that I'd be alive to see you get married," Shug said, "and I'm so happy that I can see it."

"Aw, Mum Mum. Don't make me cry."

I tried on a few dresses and I didn't like any of them. I had been trying on gowns for three hours when I saw a dress hidden on a rack that really grabbed my attention. It was white and poufy at the bottom and the veil was perfect. I went into the dressing room and tried it on. I started crying as I looked at myself in the mirror in the dressing room. I looked at my Hershey smooth skin and the womanly shape I had inherited from Jackie. The one she had before she started using. That day I knew I was beautiful despite what anybody said.

I walked out slowly and everybody's jaw dropped. Jackie started crying immediately.

"Oh my God," she said. "Come here, Melanie, let me see, let me see."

"Mom, don't start embarrassing me, please."

"Melanie, just come here, and turn around so I can see the back of the dress. You just look beautiful. Oh my God! My baby is getting married!"

Shug took a picture, and I knew I had my wedding dress.

Terron helped Lay and I decide on the colors for the wedding. After some thought, peach, black, and white were the chosen colors. Lay said whatever I wanted was fine because it was my day. That Sunday Shug invited us to church. Lay said he was coming, but he never showed up which pissed me off because he told Shug he was definitely coming. Should have been a red flag, I know.

Two months later I was late on my period. For a while I was sick and just knew I was pregnant. To my surprise I ended up getting my period and told him that I wasn't pregnant. Lay calmly said, "It's okay, baby. We will try again." We had been trying to conceive a child for a while and I was not getting pregnant.

"Lay, I'm sorry sweety, I really thought this was it, this time."

"Baby, I know and it's okay, God will give us a baby when it's time." He said rubbing my back.

I felt bad that I wasn't pregnant so I went to the doctor just to get checked out. He ran a couple routine tests and assured me I was able to conceive. I was so relieved.

I had told Lay's brother Markel about not being pregnant, and he said that he had to tell me something important about Lay because he really liked me and thought that I was cool peoples.

"Brother in law, what's up?"

"Lay is married and he can't have any more kids

because he got snipped."

"What?" I said shocked.

Then he said it again, and I hung the phone up and ran to the toilet to throw up. My body was trembling hysterically.

Jackie walked into the bathroom while I was hovering over the toilet. "Mel, what's wrong?" I had felt so humiliated. I told her what Markel had told me. She went and got the phone and called Lay's mother's house. Jackie and Ms. Lillian had talked on the phone for about an hour. When Jackie hung the phone up, she started crying.

"Baby, I am so sorry. He is married and I told his mom that y'all were planning on getting married. She assured me that he was already a married man."

Jackie held me as I cried so hard and loud that Terron came upstairs to see what was wrong. Jackie told Terron what happened, and he said that he didn't want Lay over the house anymore.

"Mel, if you marry this dude, I'm done with you," he said, putting his fist into his palm for emphasis.

I was crying so hard that I didn't even hear anything else he said after that. I thought I had the perfect guy and the perfect relationship. But it was all based on a lie.

I went into a deep depression the next couple of days. I missed class and wasn't eating the way I was supposed to. I was a total mess. My eyes were blood shot and swollen from crying so much. My heart felt so weak and empty. I hadn't heard from Lay at all for about a month. Even though he broke my heart, I still loved Lay and missed him dearly.

While we were together I had signed up for all kinds of bridal magazines and fundraisers. Magazines had started coming in the mail and my mom kept writing return to sender on each envelope and magazine. David's Bridal even called for me to pick up the wedding dress.

One day when I was lying in bed, Shug came into the room and said, "You've been sulking long enough over this man. You are still young and have your whole life ahead of you. Lay didn't expect to fall in love with you, but he did. He is a good man. He is just having trouble right now and thought you were the safety net for him. You may be his safety net, but he has to close that door before he opens one with you."

I sat up and stared at Shug as if she were crazy. Is she saying Lay's not at fault for any of this? I thought. I opened my mouth, but Shug continued.

"Now I am not saying what he did to you was right because it wasn't, but that man loves you and I have a feeling you have not seen the last of him. If you love someone let them go, and if they come back to you again, they're yours. Melanie, now you have to let him go."

"I can't," I whispered. "I still love him."

"Melanie, let him go. One day at a time, Sweetheart. Trust me, it will get easier. You may not think so now, but it will."

With each passing day, pieces of my soul started to come back together. My will power and mind got stronger and I started to do the things that I loved doing again, but I never got over Lay. He was still a good man, but he showed me the false pretenses of him. It wasn't right how he did it, and he did hurt me deeply, but I hoped that one day it would be a lesson learned on both our parts. Maybe Shug was right; maybe I hadn't seen the last of Lay.

Chapter 9

For reasons I can't even explain, Ben and I started talking again. Although I had gotten back with Ben, I constantly had Lay on my mind. It was the weirdest thing to me because I couldn't figure out the hold that Ben had over me. In my mind I was flip-flopping with my emotions for both Lay and Ben. They both had things that they did well, and things that they could get better at. As strange as it sounds, I liked Ben's edge, and Lay's smoothness. I knew I couldn't have them both, but in my mind I could. The worst part about the whole situation was thinking of Lay while I was with Ben. It could be something as simple as going to the store. I would see something that Lay liked to eat and think about him. I would randomly smell his cologne. I tried my best to play it off but to no avail. I wasn't fooling anybody. Ben noticed and didn't hesitate to ask me either.

"You thinking about dude?" he said with a hint of attitude.

"Yea," I would answer honestly and start crying.

"So then, why won't you contact him and tell him

that?"

"Because he hurt me and lied to me, I can't take him back."

"Okay, Mel but if you think you need to be with him, I'll fall back."

"No, I'm with who I want."

Around the time I got back with Ben, Shug started to get sick. She had lost her motivation to do the things she loved like cooking and going out. It was close to Christmas time and I was working at Target. I liked working there because I could use my employee discount. I was a cashier and enjoyed talking to all the customers that came in my checkout line. I had to buy Christmas gifts and was so excited because my nephew Christian was getting all these toys. He usually got everything because I spoiled him so much. It was hard for me working at Target, going to school, and taking care of a household. Ben helped me out as much as he could, providing me with the things I needed like money for clothes and my hair.

I got home one day from work and Shug called me in her room. When I walked in the room, Shug was sitting on the edge of her bed with the oxygen tank on her, wrapped in the green and white crochet blanket

that she made a few years ago. She was going over the
checklist for Christian's Christmas.

"Now Melanie, make sure that you have his Aqua
doodle, Game Cube, toy men, and did I forget
anything?"

"Mum Mum," I said, "I got all of his stuff already."

"Just making sure...please see that he has a good
Christmas."

I thought that statement was odd because she was
saying it like she wasn't going to be around.

"Melanie," Shug said, "what day is it?"

"It's Thursday, Mum Mum."

Shug started to cry. "Oh my God, Melanie I am so
scared, I don't even know what day it is. I keep losing
days."

"It's okay. I forget what day it is too sometimes."

She kept saying, "Melanie, I'm tired, my kids are
grown and on them drugs and keep fighting and
arguing, I'm just tired."

The very next day I was looking through the Target
circular. I had marked the circular up in black marker.
Then Shug said, "I was thinking about Lay today." We
were in her bedroom while she was sitting on the bed.
I continued to mark the paper up as we talked.

"I think about him all the time, wondering what he is doing, if he has someone else. He was my first love, Mum Mum."

"Baby," Shug said, "I know he hurt you and you weren't with him that long, but he was a mess."

We both laughed then she said, "You haven't seen the last of him, trust what I say."

We started to watch Monster in Law on DVD, and Shug was acting like her normal self again. While the movie was on, she didn't say anything to me. After the movie was over she started talking to me again, "I taught you how to pay bills and write checks, shop for groceries and look for sales."

"Yes you did, but why does it sound like you are going somewhere?"

She ignored me. "Your mom loves you and even though your mom is on them drugs, you are going to get her back."

"Where is all this talk coming from?" I said getting worried.

"Aw. Don't worry. It's nothing, just an old lady speaking."

Later that night, my uncles Kenny and Brandon were arguing. Everyone else was in bed sleeping. They came into Shug's room with the arguing and Shug started screaming, "Y'all are too old for this bullshit." I quickly jumped up out of bed to see what was going on.

Lately the arguing was an every night thing in the house, and it was always between them two. Who was the best son, who did what for whom. Then they started fighting and I was yelling, "Y'all want to fight, take it outside."

Shug, barely able to walk, got up and jumped in between them.

Kenny stared at Shug, anger apparent in his eyes. "Man," he said, high off drugs, "I hope you die!" Everyone just stood there stiff for a few minutes shocked as hell at what he said. I wanted to cuss him out so bad and try to smack the mess out of him, but Shug said, "Melanie, leave him alone. Don't say anything." She got in his face and said, "Motherfucker, I will show you better than I will tell you."

The arguing all of a sudden stopped and Brandon cussed out Kenny so bad. They went downstairs and lay on the couch 'cause not only were they high, but they were drunk, too. The smell of alcohol filled the room as they left.

"It don't make no sense that they argue like that. They both ain't shit. They need to just lay down and go to sleep." Shug said. "I don't know what they arguing for 'cause all of them are drug addicts and ain't do shit with their lives," she continued. "It's like they graduated high school for nothing. It's a shame when people you know come to you and say, 'oh my son is a doctor or my daughter is lawyer' and all I can say is, 'that's nice!' knowing I had four kids and they all grown and still stay with their mom and didn't amount to shit."

She turned to me and added, "Melanie, whenever you have kids, make sure you raise them right and if they get into them drugs, leave them in the street 'cause when you smother them and don't let them live on their own they will never leave."

I didn't say a word; I just listened. It hurt me to hear Shug say she was a bad mother because her children hadn't amounted to anything. The pain in her eyes hurt me so deeply.

Jackie had come in that night and let one of her friends Sherry stay the night 'cause she was tired from being out in the streets. She always appeared after the arguments.

Shug had asked Jackie, "It's cold outside. Why don't you stay home more often?"

"Mom," Jackie replied, "Tonight was my last night. I am done. I am going to change my life."

"Your daughter needs you, Jackie."

"Mom, I know and I am truly done." She said trying to sound convincing.

I had heard that same line since I was about eight years old and I wasn't holding my breath.

The next morning I had got up about six in the morning and got in the shower. I had to be to work at eight-thirty and I got up early because I had to catch two buses. Normally when I woke up, I would go into Shug's room and wake her up. We always had the best talks in the morning. But, instead I had gotten dressed first then went in to wake her up.

As I walked in the room, Shug was on the floor.

"Mum Mum, why didn't you holler or something?"

She didn't answer.

Once I realized that Shug was dead, a funny smell came across my nose. It smelled like sour milk but only worse. It was the smell of death.

I started screaming. My uncle Kenny ran upstairs.

"Mom," he screamed in between sobs.

"Call the cops," I said.

He was still screaming.

I hollered louder, "Call the cops."

When the paramedics came, they checked her out and then they had to pronounce her death. There wasn't a word to describe how I felt. Shug was the woman who raised me. My true mother was dead. It hurt me to call Shug's mother Margret to tell her that her second daughter was gone. Margret had to bury her second and last child. Then I had to call Terron and my cousins Eryc and Eryca.

While I was making the calls, I never left Shug's side. I stayed right there in the room with her and covered her with her favorite blanket. I sat there are stared at her nearly yellow complexion and her salt and pepper hair. Margret, Terron, Eryc and Eryca all came in the room while I was in a daze still holding her hand. We all cried together. We had to wait for the medical examiners to show up and move her body. About an hour later, the medical examiners showed up. They asked what time I found her.

"7:45," I answered. It hurt me to know she had been lying there all that time.

He informed the family that they had to go downstairs because they had to move the body. As I walked downstairs, I broke down.

Everyone was downstairs when my family finally came downstairs. The neighbors, other family members, and my friend Alley were all sitting downstairs. Kenny sat next to me, crying.

"I don't know why the fuck you sitting here crying," I yelled. "You just said to her last night I hope you die."

He started crying even louder. "I didn't mean it," he said through the tears.

"Whatever, you gonna say right to her face, man, 'I hope you die' and not only did she die, but ain't today your birthday, you bastard? Happy fucking birthday. This is one you will never forget."

Shug was good for calling someone a bastard, and I just copied it from her.

"So since you wanted her dead and now that she is," I continued, "why you don't bury your mother? Oh wait, you have no money."

"OK, Melanie," Eryc said, "that's enough."

I apologized to Margret because she was sitting right there while I was lashing out.

I called Lay to let him know about Shug. She was very

fond of him.

"Hey, it's Mel. I know you are wondering why I am
calling you, but…" my voice cracked.

"What's wrong?" Lay asked.

"Shug died this morning."

"Oh my God. I am so sorry. Are you ok?"

I told Lay that I was a wreck. I told him that I was
seeing my ex-boyfriend again, but I still wanted him
to come to the funeral. He told me he would feel
uncomfortable if he was there. I said okay and then
got off the phone. I wanted Lay to be with me so bad
during my time of need. I felt that I needed a really
good friend there with me, plus, I missed him.

The day of the funeral, everyone told me how good
of a job I did making the preparations for the funeral
and everything. The funeral director opened the
casket door, and there was my best friend laying
there. She looked beautiful with a baby blue dress on
and baby blue slippers. Her long hair was out, and she
had her ring on that Margret had bought her some
years ago. It was hard to finally say goodbye to her.
The funeral hall was packed and everyone was
standing waiting to view her body. Terron and I wrote

something to say about her once the body was done being viewed. Kenny, Brandon, and Jackie were there in the front crying loudly.

Her oldest son Stanly was locked up, so he came early in the morning escorted by a cop to see her. I knew that hurt him so much that he couldn't be with the family.

I walked up to Margret and held her hand. She just looked at me and smiled and said. "She's in a better place."

I nodded my head in agreement.

When the funeral was over, everyone went downstairs to the basement of the church to have the repast.

I just sat there feeling lost and wondering, What the hell am I going to do now? I couldn't stay there with my uncles and Jackie because they were still getting high and none of them had jobs. I was stuck between a rock and a hard place.

Jackie was sitting down laughing and talking with Eryca, and she said, "Melanie, are you gonna eat?"

"No, Mom, I'm not hungry."

"You have to eat something. I will fix you a plate." She gave me a hug and kissed me on the cheek. I had been waiting for that hug for fifteen years. It was sad that Shug's passing had to happen for it to occur.

The next few months were really rough. I was still working at Target only making $7.63 an hour and taking care of an entire house. By the grace of God I was paying electric, cable, telephone, and helping Terron support Christian. I was so stressed. I wasn't eating properly nor was I sleeping well. Ben was helping out when he could, but that wasn't enough. My cousin Tray was helping out too for a while, but he eventually stopped. I was frustrated.

On top of that, me and Ben had been arguing again. I was so through with Ben and him being nonchalant toward the situation. When it first started to get hectic, I could depend on him, but lately I was noticing a disturbing trend and I didn't like it. The worst part of the whole deal was that I had been feeling under the weather. I kept saying that maybe it was something I ate or maybe stressing too much. I guess deep down I knew that I was pregnant and I knew that Ben was the father. That fact mixed with him pissing me off sent me over the edge. I sat on the bed and dialed his number and waited for him to pick up the phone. When he did, I went off from the beginning.

"Ben, I can't pay these bills by myself."

"I shouldn't have to help all the time when there are grown ass men there. I mean your brother is helping but damn baby, I gotta live, too."

"I understand that, but you are living here, too."

"Melanie, I'm giving you money this last time and I'm moving out next week and you can come if you want."

"I can't move. This is my grandmother's house."

"Fine, then Melanie you stay. I'm out."

"But I'm pregnant."

There was complete silence before he responded.

"Fuck Mel, how did this happen?"

"How do you think genius?"

"I hope you ain't though," Ben said as if it was nothing.

I hung up right after he said that.

I went to the doctor with my dad. I was praying that the doctor would come in and tell me I wasn't pregnant. I was looking around and saw baby magazines, the stirrups on the examination table which scared the hell out of, me, and the bright light that was in the corner of the office. The doctor knocked on the door and then walked in. He was looking at the chart for like five minutes, which was nerve-racking and felt like 15 minutes.

Then he looked at me with a smile and said, "Miss Woodard, your pregnancy test was positive. Congratulations."

I looked at him like he was retarded and said loudly, "Positive." I put my hand on my head.

"Yes, Miss Woodard, you are approximately two months pregnant, and you conceived around December 18th."

"Well we know what you were doing on your birthday," my dad said laughing.

I just rolled my eyes at him.

The doctor said my due date was around September. I thought, Wow, Melanie, you done really did it this time. My dad was happy that he was going to be a grandfather. I was still in shock as I sat there wishing it was all a bad dream.

I am only 21, I thought. Hell I just turned 21. How am I going to take care of a baby in that house I am living in?

The nurse did a sonogram and there it was, my baby sitting there. I started crying; it looked like a little bean. The tears weren't tears of joy but tears of stupidity to get pregnant by a man who didn't want a baby.

When I got home, I called Ben on the phone and got right to it, "I am eight weeks pregnant."

"Are you serious?"

"No I'm playing, yea I'm serious and if you don't believe me I got the paper work."

"Wow Melanie eight weeks?"

"Yes, Ben eight weeks," I said, beginning to get annoyed.

"Alright do you need anything?"

"No, not right now."

"Alright, I'll be over tomorrow."

"Okay."

Jackie came in the house and saw the paperwork and prenatal vitamins on the coffee table.

"Oh my God, my daughter is pregnant."

I got up from the chair up and flatly said, "Yea, I am, Mom."

"Did you take your vitamins yet?"

"No."

Jackie went into the kitchen and returned with a glass of milk. "Take your vitamins, and I got some milk for the baby."

I took the vitamins while I rolled my eyes at Jackie because I knew that she was full of it.

"Melanie," Jackie said, "I ain't ready yet, not yet." Then she got dressed and left. I didn't see her for another two weeks.

Chapter 10

Even though I was pregnant, I still continued to go to Crozer Community College to get my degree. I hid my pregnancy the best I could just because I was ashamed at whom it was by. I was still upset that I was pregnant, but after a while I accepted it.

One day I was sitting in class and noticed that the baby hadn't moved all day. I thought maybe he was tired; I know I sure was. I had just turned eight months pregnant. Even though I was hiding my pregnancy, people knew I was pregnant. By the time I got home that afternoon, I still didn't feel the baby. A few hours later, I went to the hospital to see what was wrong.

When I arrived into the emergency room, I called my parents. I told the nurse what the emergency was and she still told me to sit in the waiting room.

"What the fuck," I yelled. "You mean to tell me that I am pregnant and I'm sitting here telling you I haven't felt my baby move all damn day and you want me to sit and wait?"

The nurse ignored me.

While I waited in the waiting room, three different

doctors came in there to tell other families that their loved ones didn't make it. I began to feel really uncomfortable and scared with all that was going on. After almost an hour of waiting, the nurse said, "Ma'am, we are seeing patients according to emergency, so please be patient."

I was ready to haul off and slap the shit out of the nurse. I waited five minutes and my parents came in together. I told them what the nurse told me. The next thing I knew, they both were hollering at the nurse. Another nurse came in and put me in the wheelchair and rushed me to the Maternity ward. Soon as I got in the room, I was getting an IV put in me.

"Ma'am," the nurse said, "your child isn't breathing."

I began to have a panic attack. A doctor rushed in the room and told me that my water was going to have to be broken and I would have to deliver my baby now.

"What is going on?" I yelled. "Is my baby going to be okay?"

Moments later, I started having contractions and my parents came in and held my hands. I was in indescribable pain. The doctor gave me some medicine to calm down the pain so I could start pushing. I was still contracting and the doctor said to the nurse, "We can't wait. We have to get this baby out now."

My parents had called Ben while they were in the waiting room and of course he didn't pick up. The doctor, the nurse, and my parents all were yelling, "Push, Melanie, push."

The pain was so devastating but I did what I was told. By that time I had pushed two more times then stopped.

"I don't want to do this," I screamed. "My baby is dead. I still don't feel anything."

Tears rolled down my cheeks like a water faucet. I was told to push again. I had pushed another three times and out came a baby that was blue with the umbilical cord stuck around his neck. Immediately Jackie started screaming.

I was in shock, sitting there looking at my deceased son. I looked like I was a patient at a psychiatric center, so lost, like I didn't know where I was.

Fifteen minutes later, the doctor came in telling me that he was sorry, that he did all he could do.

"I want my baby!" I yelled, crying hysterically. "I want my baby now!"

Jackie rocked me back and forth as I cried. My dad sat

there, in shock. I knew he wanted to alleviate the pain
for me, but he wasn't able to. Then he held both
Jackie and me as he began to cry with us.
"If that nurse didn't make me wait in the emergency
room all that time," I told my parents, "my baby
would have been here. Mom, I believe that."
Jackie didn't say anything. She just sat on the bed
next to me in a daze.
The nurse bought the baby out to me. He looked just
like Ben, same ears, mouth, and hands. I held him for
a quick second, then I couldn't take it anymore. My
body felt numb, and I wasn't able to control my
crying. My parents held him and they took pictures. I
didn't want a picture at all. The doctor spoke to my
parents about funeral arrangements, and what they
wanted done to the body. Before I cried myself to
sleep, I told my mom that I was naming him Benjamin
Woodard. I named him after his dad even though he
didn't deserve it. It was the quickest name that came
to mind.

My family gave Benjamin a home-going
ceremony. The ceremony was in a small church. There
was a piano on the far right with a microphone next to
the pulpit. A few of my family and friends were

already sitting. As I was walking down the aisle,
everyone's eyes were on me. Ben had the nerve to
show up and of course I made a scene.

"For someone who didn't give a damn about his son,
why you come here now?" I yelled.

Ben sighed. "Melanie, I don't want to argue with you
today."

I rolled my eyes at him. I was so pissed that I told
Jackie to tell the funeral coordinator to not let him see
our son.

"I am not doing that," Jackie said. "Even though he
wasn't there, that is still his son and he is grieving just
like you are, baby."

She had a point but, I still didn't want him there.
When I looked up at the front of the church, there was
a small blue casket that held my son. I was so
distressed that I couldn't even get an outfit for him;
Jackie handled all of that. I had gotten him a blue
pajama set with trains on it. He had a bib that read I
love my Mommy and Daddy, and a blue rattle in his
hand. People were viewing the body and coming up
hugging me and Ben.

Then it was my turn to go up, and Ben tried to go up
with me, but I hurried up and grabbed my father. I

looked at my son and cried my heart out. When I screamed, my father and Ben tried their best to calm me down.

I told Jackie that I wished Lay was the father.

"I know you do," Jackie said. "You said that as soon as you told me you were pregnant. Melanie, everything happens for a reason. Lay wasn't supposed to be the father."

Ben cried as he went up to the casket. My dad went up with him and held his shoulder. I knew the guilt had set in.

I thought, He just ought to cry.

That night Ben came over and I was lying in bed with the TV on. He touched my leg and I jumped in fear. But for some reason when I saw him, I hugged him and started crying. Then I was hitting him and crying. When I got myself together, I asked him, "Why did you leave me when I needed you the most? I mean I knew we weren't getting back together, but I was carrying your child."

"I left you because I was scared and didn't know what to do," he said avoiding eye contact.

"That is the dumbest shit I have ever heard, but if that is your story, you stick to it because I ain't buying that."

He sucked his teeth at me. "See, Melanie, I can't talk to you." He stormed out of the room. He was always good for avoiding a confrontation.

"I swear," I said, "all I ever see is his back.

Chapter 11

The day had finally come when I got my own apartment. It was the best feeling ever. I got a one bedroom and it was just enough for me. Jackie was upset that I was moving because she didn't want me to leave. But I wasn't moving far, and I knew she was going to be over all the time. She was over my house every day eating all the food in my refrigerator, coming in off her crack binges. Even though I hated the fact that my mother did get high, I still loved her and always fed her. Shug always taught me to never deprive anyone of food because God came in different shapes and sizes.

One day I left Jackie at my house because I was leaving to help Margret. Me, Eryc, Eryca, Bingo, and Muja went over to her house to clean up for inspection. She lived in an apartment where they did inspection almost every year. We had to mop her floors, clean out closets, refrigerators, bathroom, and the bedrooms. You name it, it was being cleaned. Margaret was the type to not throw away anything. While we were cleaning up, she sat in her living room in her black leather chair watching the movie Repo.

While she was watching the movie, she nodded off to sleep, but when anyone threw something in the trash can, she would wake up and say, "Don't throw that away."

We were there for a few hours. Once we were finished cleaning, she thanked us for getting everything ready, and we kissed her and told her goodnight.

✳✳✳✳✳

Terron had come over my house to stay the night with me one weekend. We lay in the bed and were talking for hours about any and everything just like we used to do when we were younger. We reminisced about how Shug would take us to Cow Town just about every Saturday. Cow Town was located in New Jersey and it had different barns that sold almost anything you could think of.

He bought up the fact that Shug hadn't left the house to anyone. "Melanie, I was thinking about trying to get Mum Mum's house."

"You were?" I said, shocked.

"Yea and I want your name on the deed, too."

"Terron, I am not getting caught up in one of your scams. You won't have me sitting in jail looking crazy over your bullshit."

One thing about Terron, he would try to work his way into some kind of scam like making up a fake business to get loans. If he wanted something done that was all there was to it. Then he showed me these papers with forged signatures on them with his sloppy handwriting.

"Terron," I said, "you are going to jail." He just laughed at me and then went to sleep.

Terron was sick with a heart problem, so while he was sleeping I would watch him. He started to snore loudly which annoyed me to no end. But I loved Terron very much, so I put up with it. As I was watching him sleep, he looked so peaceful holding the white pillow as he lay on his side. I missed spending time with Terron since I had moved, so I enjoyed his company. Had I known that it was going to be our last time talking, I would have said a whole lot more to him.

One day I was at work when I got the phone call. My friend and co-worker Missie had told me my mother was on the phone. I got on the phone and Jackie was crying so loudly I couldn't make out what she was saying to me.

Finally, Jackie calmed down enough to tell me that

Terron had died.

"Stop playing," I said waiting for the joke to end. I knew Terron had a heart problem, but he was only 31. After she repeated it, I sat there with the work phone in my hand in a daze. I still didn't believe my mother; I was at a loss for words.

I called Terron's cell phone and left a message for him to call me. Then I called his friend Tony's house. He answered the phone, sounding frantic. I told him to put Terron on the phone.

"My mom said he died," I said, "but I told her to stop smoking that shit." I said forcing a laugh.

"Melanie," Tony said, his voice cracking, "he did die." I cried even harder. I sobbed and listened to Tony, who explained to me what happened. He said that Terron went to the club and came in the house drunk. Then he said he went to the bathroom because his stomach hurt.

Tony said he asked Terron if he were OK, and Terron said he was fine. Then he told me when he came downstairs that morning, Terron was on the floor naked and he had lost his bowels. After I explained to my boss about Terron, he told me to go home.

Ashya, another co-worker of mine, took me to Shug's

house. No one was at Shug's so I walked around the
corner to Terron's paternal grandma's house. When I
walked in the house, Jackie was sitting on the couch
crying and I just held her close. I felt so bad for Jackie
because she lost her son. All I could think about was
the loss of another best friend. I had never felt so
alone.

The funeral was a nice ceremony. Terron had written
his own obituary and saved it on my computer. It
made me wonder if he knew all along that he was
going to die soon. He was weird like that, into dead
people and stuff. Terron's home-going was a two-day
affair. Terron had on a nice black suit with the hat
that he always wore, and nice black shoes. He also had
on a pink, black, and white tie.
 There were eight hours' worth of singing and it was so
comforting. A lot of people just walked up and were
singing his favorite songs. Jackie and I sat in the
second row and his wife Shelia sat with us. Terron
also had two children by his wife, Calvin and Brian.
The church was so packed that people were standing.
I hadn't realized that Terron knew so many people.
There were different choirs singing and people

coming up talking about Terron. He was really loved.
The next day was the burial. Terron was a veteran; he
served in the Army, so they had to bury him at the
Veteran's Cemetery. There weren't too many people at
the burial, but that was fine. I felt bad for all my
nephews though. The person that was hosting the
burial said a few words, and then he did the salute and
gave Shelia the flag. The family all received flowers
and then marched out.

As I was in line leaving out of the room the ceremony
was held in, I touched Terron's casket to say my final
goodbye to my brother.

Chapter 12

One day I decided to walk to work and I saw this guy; to me, he wasn't good looking at all. But he paid me some attention, so I thought I'd see what he was about. I wished that I never spoke to him and kept on walking to work.

His name was Marcus, he was tall and light skin. Marcus was 6'2 with green eyes and a small scar under his left eye. He was shaped like a pencil, thin and straight. But two things I did like about Marcus was that his nails were clean and he had decent conversation.

I dealt with Marcus because I was vulnerable and Marcus saw that. There were so many red flags that I ignored because I didn't want to be alone. Marcus and I started talking, and I had told him about the various deaths in my family. Marcus seemed really sincere at the time. We talked a lot and took walks in the park which I loved.

One day in particular, Marcus and I decided to walk in the park. It was a beautiful day, the sky was clear, and the birds were chirping. We found a park bench and sat down.

After a moment of silence, I said, "Marcus."

"Yes, Mel."

"Tell me a little more about you."

"Uh, like what that I don't have anywhere to live?"

"Why not?" I asked, caught off guard.

"My parents moved to North Carolina," he said looking away from me.

"Aww, I'm sorry to hear that. You can stay with me if you like," I said turning his face toward mine.

"I don't want to intrude."

"I could use the company." I smiled.

"Okay."

If I were in my right mind, that would have been a red flag right there. A grown ass man with nowhere to live. For a few months, everything was great. We talked, went out, and did things couples did until Marcus's true colors came to the surface.

Eventually Marcus had stopped going to work, so he lost his job. While I went to work and school, he was at my house, claiming he was looking for work. Of course I believed him.

Jewel had told me about a job opening at Staples. When I got home, I told Marcus about the job and for

him to apply. He applied for the job on the internet
and ended up getting the job only to work for two
damn weeks. One day he just didn't show up to work
and was fired. I felt I should have left him, but I
didn't.

Jackie would call every day just like any mother
would and asked what was going on with Marcus. I
lied for him and said he was helping out with bills
when he really wasn't. It had gotten so bad that he had
women call my house and told them he was single. We
argued almost every night, and that was when the
abuse started.

The first time he hit me, he got mad because I
wouldn't give him money. I thought, What is this
motherfucker getting on? I mean I know he smoked
weed but damn was he smoking hard too? In that
instant I kept a close watch on my purse, jewelry, and
other belongings; it was clearly time for him to go.
But, because I didn't want to be alone, he stayed.
One night I had to call the cops on Marcus. I was off
work that day.
We had a good day so far when the arguing started
about his shirt that shrunk in the dryer. Once the two
of us started arguing about the shirt, I knew he was

seeing someone else or at least fucking someone else.
Who argues about a shirt?

Marcus hit me in my ribs and I swung back,
connecting with his chin barely. Then he punched me
in the face and dragged me across the floor from my
bedroom to my living room. Constantly he kicked me
in my ribs while I did my best to shield my body. Then
I got the strength to get up and I just started swinging
on him nonstop. The end result was him leaving that
night and me hoping he was safe.

The abuse went on for about two months too long. But
I still managed to go to work, keep my grades up, and
maintain the bills.

I thought to myself enough was enough. I deserved
better than what I was getting. Marcus not only
abused me mentally, physically, emotionally, but I lost
myself over a man who was clearly not worth it.

I soon started to put things in perspective, and I had
to get my life back on track. I knew that I didn't love
Marcus. The sex completely stopped, and not only was
he old news but he was definitely bad news. I thought
I could see a good side of Marcus and sometimes I
did. I thought that I could change him but I couldn't.
One morning Marcus wanted to have sex and I told

him no. He got mad and left the house and came back within two hours. He was high and drunk. I was in the bed sleeping. He came in the room and sat down on the edge of the bed. I woke up scared, wondering if he was going to try something. But he didn't, he just woke me up and apologized for the arguing, hitting, and pain that he had caused me. I didn't buy it one bit. I sat up and told him that he had to go because I had enough and the relationship wasn't working at all. I could see the rage in his eyes building up. He just said, "Okay, I understand."

"You have to leave, Marcus."

"Ok, but can I get my things tomorrow?"

"Yes, but if you don't come get them, I'm throwing all of it away," I said meaning every word. I sat up and watched him walk out of the dark room. After I was sure he was gone, I lay back down and tried my hardest to go back to sleep.

When I woke up to get ready for work, something said, "Check your wallet." All of my money was gone and my keys, too.

I was pissed off at myself for leaving it out. When I noticed that my wallet was missing, I wondered why I was going through so much pain and agony. I sat on my couch, picked up my brown bible off my glass table and began reading. I didn't know what verse or scripture I was reading, but as I started to read the tears fell.

The feeling of emptiness filled my heart. I had hardly any family left, no boyfriend that cared for me, and no sense of who I was. While I was crying, I began to pray. I prayed for peace, clarity, and the ability to find my way because I had been so lost for so long. When I finished praying, I called maintenance from the apartment building and immediately got locks changed. I wasn't too mad about the money because money comes and it goes. Then I got up and took all of Marcus's belongings and threw them out the window. I called my mom and dad about my money being stolen. They were pissed. My parents had been fed up with Marcus, but they taught me that I had to live my own life. My dad drove around in his truck to see if he could find him. There was no sign of Marcus. I felt so much better and relieved that he was finally out of my life. It was the worst relationship that I had ever been in. Not only had I lost my sense of self with him, but I lost a lot of weight, which normally would have pleased me, but it just made me more upset. I just thanked God that I never got pregnant by Marcus. I don't think I could have handled that.

Chapter 13

Being single made me think a lot about me. I learned not to settle when I was worth so much more. It wasn't fair that some men would take advantage of a woman when she was at her most vulnerable state. I put Marcus behind me and was glad that I did. I had gained my strength back and was able to be Mel again. My depression had gone away and the doctor said that I didn't need any more depression pills.

One night I was fiddling on MySpace. Browsing through pages, I had come across a lot of people that I went to high school with, and I added them as my friends. Lay was heavy on my mind, so I decided to see if he had a MySpace page. I typed in his name in the Delaware slot, he wasn't there. Then I typed his name in to the VA slot and his picture popped up. When I saw that picture, my heart started pounding. I began to have butterflies in my stomach as I stared at the picture.

I sat there with my mouth wide open because I couldn't believe it was him. I couldn't believe I found the man that I had fallen in love with. I was at the computer for about fifteen minutes contemplating if I should send him a friend request. I wondered if he were back with his wife, if he had a girlfriend, or if he would even talk to me. Then I remembered Shug saying, "You have not seen the last of Lay."

"I am still in love with him," I whispered and quickly hit the add friend button.

After the request was sent, I got up from my computer, pacing back and forth as I wondered if he was going to add me or even send me a message.

A part of me was thinking that he would come over my house, hold me, make love to me, and we would sleep the night away. The other part of me was thinking that he didn't want me and he had moved on with someone else. I began to get frantic, so I poured myself a glass of wine. I sat at the computer for an hour checking just to see if he added me. Waiting at the computer, my back started to get stiff, and my hands began to sweat. I was so nervous waiting for Lay to get back to me that I fell asleep right at the computer.

The next morning I woke up and quickly logged into my MySpace account. When I checked to see who my new friends were, Lay was there. I ran around the house like I had just hit the lottery. I looked into my inbox and saw where he left a message.

The message stated:

Hey there, Miss Lady.

As soon as I read that part, I was smiling hard from ear to ear 'cause I loved when he called me that.

How have u been? Call me. My number's below. We need to talk.

My heart was beating a mile a minute while I wrote his number down.

I thought, Okay I am not going to call him now, I will call him when I get off work tonight.

Work was going by so slow and I could not wait to get home so I could call him. Soon as I was done counting out the cash register, I got on the bus to get home. When I got home, I grabbed the phone and took the number out of my pocket. Then I sat there and stared at it.

"Okay," I said, "I can do this." Then I said, "No I can't, who I am kidding? He is probably in love with someone else." Finally I got the nerve then dialed the number.

"Hello," a voice answered.

"Hello, can I speak to Lay, please?"

"Speaking."

"Hey, Lay, it's Melanie, how are you?"

"Hey, Miss Lady, I'm good, how are you doing?"

I started smiling from ear to ear all excited. Then there was an awkward silence between us. It was the kind of silence that you have when you first meet someone. I started having flashbacks of my abusive relationship with Marcus and wished Lay was there to save me.

"Melanie, I always thought about you," he said, sounding sincere.

"Really?"

"Yes."

"You know I still think about that terrible stunt you pulled that broke my heart."

"I know you do, and I am truly sorry, I was going through a tough time."

"That's what they all say."

"It's the truth, Mel," he said as his voice rose a little.

"Lay, I don't even know what that means coming from your mouth."

"I deserve that."

"Anyway what's new with you?" I said trying to

change the subject.

"Nothing much, I'm divorced now."

"Really?"

"Yea, I got divorced right after we broke up."

There was that awkward silence again.

"So how are the kids?"

"They're doing fine."

Lay and I talked all night catching up and telling each other what we had been through since we were apart. I told him about Marcus and Lay listened without interrupting me once. I started crying while I was talking to Lay because it all was a little overwhelming. That coupled with the abusive relationship that I was in with Marcus and now reuniting with the man that I never fell out of love with. Lay was like Velcro; I stuck to him no matter what.

Lay and I started spending a lot of time with each other and just talking about our past and history that we had. We spent time with Lay's children and his family. His children were the sweetest kids ever. Lay had four beautiful children. I spoiled them all rotten. Me, Lay and the kids went to the mall, park, and out to eat. We were just like one big happy family.

I loved Lay's mother so much. Lillian was a
sweetheart. She would give anyone her last if they
needed it. We called each other and talked about
different things whether it was the love of God or what
we were cooking for dinner. We went out to movies
and had dinners at her house. Our relationship had
definitely improved for the better.

Being involved with his family made me remember
what my family used to be. Jackie was excited when I
told her that I was talking with Lay again, but she also
said for me to be careful.

Just when everything was going right between
Lay and I, the devil stepped in and
tried to do his dirty work.

One day when I was at work, my boss Billy handed me
an envelope.

"Billy, where did you get this from?"

"It was mailed here, Miss Melanie," Billy said.

I opened it and read the threatening letter that stated
that Marcus had owed some people money. As I was
reading, I thought, What in the hell does this have to
do with me? It said that if I didn't get in contact with
Marcus, these people were going to kill him and they
knew where I lived. The only part I was concerned

about was that they knew where I lived.

Right away I took the letter to the County police. The county police made copies of the letter and told me to go to the state police. I did what I was told and the cops asked me if I thought I knew who it was. I said to the cops, "I think it's my ex boyfriend, Marcus." I called and told my parents and Lay about the letter. Of course my parents were furious with Marcus at this point and I was terrified. I had to get rides to and from work and school in case Marcus was stalking me. I was upset because I was putting my life on the line for a crazy ex-boyfriend who didn't want to grasp the concept that it was over. I ended up filing a restraining order on Marcus but not before I received a few more letters. Then all of a sudden, the threats died down. I had truly learned a lesson, to always follow my instincts about people no matter what. I felt like I was a better person for going through it.

Chapter 14

It had been a long day and to tell the truth I was bored. I was coming in my house from the grocery store on a Saturday morning when I heard my phone ringing.

"Hello," I said, setting the groceries on the table.

"Hi, Miss Melanie." It was Layla, Lay's youngest daughter.

"Hey, sweetie, how are you?"

"I'm doing okay. I wanted to know if me and Lanisha can come over your house when Daddy comes?"

"Sure, sweetheart, you girls are always welcome."

"Yay, thanks, Miss Melanie."

"Okay, Layla, see you soon, sweetie."

"Bye," she said.

"Hey Miss Lady."

I smiled at the sound of Lay's voice. "Hey Baby, what's up?"

"Nothing, getting the kids dressed."

"Where is Layton, Jr. and Layaire?"

"Playing their video games."

"Oh ok. Well baby, I'm 'bout to get this lasagna started and I'll see you in about an hour."

"Alright, sweetie, see you then."

"I love you."

"Love you too, Baby."

After hanging up the phone, I got all the groceries out of the bags and began preparing the lasagna.

"Where is that damn ricotta cheese?" I asked, rustling through the bags. "Ah found it!"

Once the lasagna was done, I put the lasagna in the center of the table with the garlic bread. While waiting for them to arrive, I started reading OK magazine and hadn't gotten through the first couple pages, when the door bell interrupted me. I put the magazine down and opened the door. There stood Lay, Layla and Lanisha. Layla always greeted me with the biggest hugs.

"Miiissss Melanie!" Layla said, extending her arms toward me.

"Hey Layla. Oh my goodness you and your big hugs!"

Lanisha wasn't as enthusiastic as her sister. I guess that's how it was when you're fifteen.

"Hey Miss Melanie," Lanisha said just above a whisper.

"Hey Lanisha."

Lay gave me a hug after Lanisha did.

"I missed you, baby."

"Aawww me too sweetie," I said holding the embrace as tight as I could as I inhaled his cologne.

"Miss Melanie."

"Yes Lanisha."

"It smells good in here."

"Thanks, sweetie. I made lasagna."

Lay and the kids took off their coats and sat down to the dinner table. I went in the kitchen and grabbed the pitcher of iced tea.

"Baby, I'm 'bout to tear this food up," Lay said, grabbing his fork.

"Boy, you are a mess."

"Daddy, save some for us," the girls said in unison.

Lay leaned over and kissed me in front of the girls which made me blush. I didn't like it when he did that around the kids because even though they liked me, I didn't want to confuse them.

After having dinner and laughing with Lay and the kids, I began cleaning up with the girls' help. Layla wanted to do the dishes and Lanisha wanted to dry them while I wiped down the table and stove. Lay was in the living room watching the football game.

"Miss Melanie, how do you know when a boy likes

you?"

Lanisha was asking the wrong person I thought to myself.

"Well it all depends. Does he act different around you?"

"Miss Melanie, he stutters every time he talks to me now, and he has never done that before."

"Well then I think he does."

"Don't tell my dad though, okay?" She glanced over at Lay.

"Okay, I won't," I said, winking.

"Okay, Miss Melanie," she said, smiling.

Once we finished cleaning up, Lay got up and got ready to take the girls home.

"Girls, get your coats on. It's time to go," he said, cutting the TV off.

They both grabbed their coats from the hall closet.

"Do we have to go?" Layla said, pouting.

"Layla, what did I say?" Lay said grilling her.

"Okay Dad, don't have a baby."

We all laughed so hard.

"Sweetie," Lay said to me, "I'm going to take them home, and I'll call you later."

"Alright," I said, giving Lay a quick peck on his lips.

"Girls, call me later, ok?"
"Okay, Miss Melanie," they both said.

After Lay and the kids left, I got ready for bed. I appreciated the time that I spent with Lay and the kids. I felt like I had my own family if only for one night. That feeling was something that always crossed my mind. I got into bed that night feeling great. I felt like things were going the way they were supposed to for a change.

Chapter 15

The last semester of college finally came, and I was so excited. I was about to start my second internship at Tender Loving Care, Incorporated, a school for pregnant students to attend to learn child care and academics. All that was on my mind was passing so I could finally graduate. I had been at College Diamond Community College for about four years now. With all things considering in my life as far as the deaths in my family and me losing my son, I never dropped out of school. It felt special to even be at this point.

I walked into the front door of TLCI and signed in at the main office; Josie the secretary greeted me. Josie was a 5 foot, white, thin girl almost like Paris Hilton in appearance had a very eager spirit. She talked really fast, which made me very overwhelmed. Josie was telling me that I had to host a group and do all of these tedious assignments like clean the microwave, go through files, and re-type everything that was in them. I did what I was told because I knew that at the end of my experience I was receiving something greater.

At 11:00 am that day I sat in what was supposed to be
a cafeteria to hold group. I was waiting patiently while
the students came in with their bellies wobbling. I
started to get a little worried because these girls were
adolescents and not only that they were pregnant and
hormonal. There were five girls that came down.
While the girls were sitting in a circle in their chairs, I
introduced myself as an intern. They all just looked at
me, bored. I saw the tension that was building so
when I finished the introduction, I said, "Okay today
you all can pick the topic for the group. Whatever you
guys want to talk about is fine with me."
They immediately got excited. The girls decided to
talk about how they felt about being pregnant. The
topic was comfortable because everyone could relate,
even me. One student shared her experience and then
everyone was getting involved. But one of the girls was
quiet and didn't share anything. I thought right away
that I had to pay a little more attention to her.
It was 4:00 pm and I was gathering up my things
getting ready to leave. Josie came up to me and asked,
"So, how was your first day?"
"I loved it," I responded, "and the girls responded to
me quickly which was great."

Josie leaned in and whispered, "That's good but you have to watch out for the staff here. They go around talking about everyone and Velvet, she watches you like a hawk."

I didn't respond to Josie's comment. I listened, told her to have a good evening, and left the building.

As the months went by, I discovered that there was a lot of drama going on behind the scenes at TLCI, but the students stayed consistent. I spoke to my advisors about the frustrations that I was having so I did have support through my school. I continued to keep my head up and still do the best that I could. In my mind I kept thinking and saying, the end result: graduate with your degree.

One day while I was at TLCI, a student's family member passed away. I felt bad for the student because I knew firsthand about losing a loved one. The girl showed so much strength within herself because even though she was going through this loss, she continued to come to school and participate in the groups that were being held. The girl came to me and asked if I would go to the funeral to support her because she felt comfortable with me. I said that I would.

Through Her Eyes

The day of the funeral was a little rough because I
knew the feeling of losing someone close to you. I
actually knew it all too well. Thoughts of little Ben
flooded my mind and the sight was crystal clear. I
could see his little face and for a moment I wondered
what life would have been like had he still been alive. I
sat outside the church staring at the cross that hung
above the double doors. I closed my eyes and said a
prayer to calm me down.

I opened the car door, got out, and brushed myself off
before walking in. The setting was so serene as I
walked up the carpeted aisle. Once I got a few feet
from the front door, I spotted the student sitting with
her father. I walked up to her and gave her a
comforting hug. A few moments after that, it was time
for the viewing. I walked slowly up to the pink casket
and paused as I viewed the body. I bowed my head
and said a quick prayer before I turned around and
walked back toward the student. I gave her another
hug and let her know it would be alright. I held her
and rocked her back and forth. I felt like so much like
a mother it was unreal. While I held her I cried. I cried
for my son Benjamin. I cried for my grandmothers
and my brother. But most of all I cried for the

student's loss. I tried my best to straighten up before I left but I knew I was a mess. The experience turned out to be more emotionally draining than I thought. The first thing I wanted to do was go home and get some rest.

Monday morning I was doing an assignment for Velvet when I was called into the office.

"Did you attend a funeral with a student?" she asked, reclining in her chair.

"Yes."

"It was told to me that you told the student that you would go."

"No, I was asked if I could go to the funeral," I said feeling uneasy.

"We can't have an intern that has been that close to clients especially outside of the facility."

I was in shock at what I was hearing. I didn't think that it was fair at all that the student switched my words around.

"I'm sorry, Melanie, but I'm terminating your internship," she said, almost smiling. I felt like this was a repeat of high school. Here I am trying to do well and be nice to people and I am still punished for trying to be the nice person.

I sat there dumbfounded. I went to my office and quickly grabbed my things. I tried my best to hold my emotions in check. I didn't want anybody to see me break down. While I was gathering my belongings, Josie asked me, "Hey Mel, what's wrong?"

"I'm no longer going to be interning here," I said, fighting back the tears. After I said that I walked past her and exited the building.

A few days later I had a meeting with my advisors about the whole ordeal. We were in the conference room and the expressions on their faces didn't make me feel the slightest bit comfortable. I was hoping the decision would be overturned. That hope went out the window when one of my advisors spoke up.

"Melanie, I'm sure you already know why you have been called here."

"Yes, ma'am."

"In your case Melanie you clearly violated policy which is stated on the documents you signed when you first joined us. With that in mind it is the opinion of this advisory board that you be given a failing grade because of this."

"Is there anything I can do to make this right?" I said pleading.

"I'm afraid not. We have to stand by our policy when
it comes to matters of these kind. I'm sorry Melanie."
It was clear that they had made up their mind. I
couldn't even think clearly. I was glad when I was able
to leave and get as far away from them as I could.
I was so disappointed in myself and the whole
situation. I thought that I was being there for a
student in her time of need because I could relate to
what she was going through. Had I known that I was
not only going to fail the internship, but not graduate
either, clearly I would have taken a different
approach. With the situation that I experienced, I felt
terrible about my actions. I began to pray to God
about the next chapter in my life, and I was confident
He would guide me through.

Chapter 16

I started to see some changes in Lay. It was a Friday night when Lay was watching the Lakers game. His eyes were glued to the TV set, and I walked up and tried to get a kiss from him. He brushed me off and said, "Honey, I'm watching the game."

Yea, I thought. I know you always watch the game.

I went into the kitchen and started to cook dinner. I was cooking curry chicken, something I knew he would eat because Lay was always a picky eater.

Dinner was done and I made our plates and sat them on the table where we always ate at.

"Sweetie, since the game is on, I'm going to eat in front of the TV," he said not taking his eyes off the game.

I just gave him his plate, and we sat on the couch and ate. Within three minutes of Lay eating the meal, he said in disgust, "What the hell is this?"

I looked at him like he was retarded. I said, "Uh, it's curry chicken."

"Well it don't taste right." His face wrinkled.

Now all of a sudden it doesn't taste right, I thought. I made it lots of times, and it was good.

Lay got up from the brown couch and threw the food in the trash can.

"Well," I said, "since you don't want to eat, you can go back home and eat there."

He walked back to the couch, sat, and continued watching the game. I was pissed off. Not only did I feel unappreciated but Lay didn't buy that food I cooked. In rage with fire bubbling inside me, I got up and turned off the TV.

"Why did you do that?" Lay asked.

"Well, since you didn't pay for the food I cooked and don't like it all of a sudden, then you don't get to watch the cable that I pay for either." I folded my arms and stood in the front of the TV.

Lay copped an attitude. He tried to turn back on the TV, but I snatched the remote from him. I went in my bedroom and started to write in my journal. A few moments later Lay walked in.

"Mel, I'm sorry for snapping about the food," he said, leaning against the doorway. He then dug in his pocket and handed me $50 to replace the chicken.

"I'm still mad, Lay, but this money makes me feel a little better," I said with a half smile.

Later that night, Lay was lying on the couch watching

TV and I wanted some quality time. I started to kiss Lay and he was not showing affection back to me yet again. Our sex life had hit rock bottom. We hadn't made love in two months.

I knew something wasn't right. First the food, now the sex. So I told Lay that I was going to bed, and Lay said that he was going to sleep on the couch.

Lay and I had gotten distant. He stopped coming over, but we still talked on the phone. I was talking to my friend from school and she had invited me to go to church. I had been so stressed from the school situation and Lay. In the church there were people hugging me and welcoming me to the church. Sitting in the church pew, I was listening to what the pastor was saying about love and relationships, and I began to cry. All I could think about was my so called relationship with Lay. In the back of my mind I knew that it was over between us. I knew that the relationship wasn't going anywhere.

I sat there and listened to the choir sing a song called "Grateful" by Hezekiah Walker and the tears were streaming down my face. People were hugging me and rubbing my back letting me know that they were there for me. I felt the anointing that was filling in the air.

Later that night I asked Lay to come over so we could talk about our relationship. He came over and sat on the couch. I looked at Lay in his gorgeous brown eyes and spoke from my heart when I said, "Lay, I love you."

"Mel," Lay said, "why do you love me?"

I sat next to him on the couch and responded, "Well, you opened your heart to me and gave me a chance. You let me meet your family, your kids, and your kids' mother and I know that wasn't an easy thing for you to do.

"I feel special because you can open your heart to me and let me in while telling me the truth about everything the second time around."

The way Lay looked at me he didn't have to speak one word.

"Why can't you love me?" I asked.

"Mel, it's not that I don't love you. I only love you as a friend."

My facial expression changed from happiness to sadness. I stood quiet for a few seconds. I wanted to punch him square in the face. I spoke with tears in my eyes, "A friend? You only love me as a friend after all we have been through? Lay, I had been with you a long time and you only love me as a friend?"

"Mel, you want children and I can't provide that for you," he said, sounding defeated.

"You didn't even try to see what options you had to have children."

When he didn't respond, I added, "Since you only love me as a friend, that's all we will be. Now get all your shit and get the fuck out my house."

He gathered his things while I sobbed on the couch. Lay tried to console me, but I just pushed him off me. "Get out," I screamed. "Get out."

A few minutes later Lay had all his things packed and he tried to hug me again, but I didn't budge. He kissed me on the lips and I still didn't move. He finally grabbed his things off the table and left.

After he was gone I got into the bathtub. I felt like my heart had been broken in half and stomped on. Sitting in the bath tub, I kicked and screamed and asked God, "Why did I let him hurt me again?"

When I finished putting my night clothes on, I began to pray to God in hopes of healing my pain. As I was praying, my phone kept ringing and I knew it was Lay. By the thirteenth call, I picked the phone up. "What?"

"Mel, I'm sorry," Lay said. "I never meant to hurt you,

but all I can say is that I tried, but I don't love you the way you love me. You want children and I know that I am not capable of providing that for you. Mel, you didn't fail, I was the one that failed you. My heart won't let me forget about you.

"You deserve someone who is going to love and cherish you. Someone who will give you what your heart desires, and your heart desires a child. Mel, I see how you glow when you are with my children. How do you think I feel when people say Mel, when you going to have kids? I don't want you to settle."

"Forget my number and leave me alone," I said then hung up the phone.

I sat on my bed with my bible in my hand absorbing all that Lay had to say. I was still pissed and couldn't believe he did this to me. Finally I cried myself to sleep with the bible lying next to me.

For the next few weeks Lay was still calling me and I ignored his calls. I continued to go to church and worship God. Although it was hard dealing with the break up, I still kept God first.

✶✶✶✶✶

I was checking my instant messenger on AOL and I had a message from Lay.

Lay: How you been?

Melanie: I'm taking one day at a time. Time heals all wounds even the ones that men put on women.

Lay: I deserve that.

Melanie: Does she cook and wash your clothes, too?

Lay: No, I cook, too, but she does wash both our clothes.

Tears formed in my eyes.

Melanie: What? Wow, it's been a few weeks since we broke up and you already moved on and you living with that bitch. I sighed. I'm sorry. She's not a bitch. Just crazy, that's all. Well, I hope that she was a good catch.

Lay didn't respond.

Melanie: Don't talk to me ever again, I added. Forget about me, okay.

Then I signed off instant messenger and deleted my account. I sat on my bed with tears strolling down my face when my cell phone rang. It was Lillian, Lay's mother.

"Hey Honey, how you doing?"

"I just finished talking to your son who has moved on with another woman," I said.

"Are you serious? Melanie, I didn't know that. He just

told me that he was going on a trip and he would be back."

"Well she's the trip he's taken," I said sarcastically.

"Mel," she said, "I thought yawl was going to get married and be happy."

"So did I, Miss Lillian, but things don't work out like we plan."

"You watch. That woman ain't like you. You are truly loved and were there for my son. You are perfect for my son, Melanie."

"Well, he don't think so. I'm done with him."

Lillian's voice was cracking and it sounded like she was about to cry.

"Miss Lillian, I have to go."

"I understand, baby, you keep in touch okay?"

"Yes, ma'am," I said hanging up the phone.

A YEAR LATER

It was Monday morning when my alarm woke me out of a deep sleep. I quickly hit the snooze button and got up to start my day. My cell phone rang and scared the hell out of me as I got out of shower.

"Hello."

"Well, well, look who answers her phone."

"Who the fuck is this?"

"I miss fucking that pussy at night."

"Who is this?" I said beginning to get scared.

"Who do you think it is, baby? It's Marcus, I know we have been out of touch for awhile, but you could never stay away from me."

My mind was in panic mode.

"Goodbye, Marcus, I'm calling the cops."

After I hung up on him, I dialed 911 while my call waiting was beeping.

"911, what's your emergency?"

"Umm yes, can you connect me to Detective Anderson?"

"Ma'am, is there a problem?"

"Put Detective Anderson through please," I said with a little more authority.

"Yes, Ma'am please hold."

"Detective Anderson speaking, how can I help you?"

"Detective Anderson, this is Melanie Woodard.
Marcus just called me and I'm scared."

"Miss Woodard, calm down."

"What the fuck you mean calm down. He all of a
sudden is calling me after a year!"

"Miss Woodard, I am going to put an APB out on
Marcus and try to get him in for questioning. I will
call you when I hear something. Meanwhile don't go
anywhere alone and be careful."

"Okay, thank you, Detective Anderson and I'm sorry
for cussing at you."

"It's fine, Miss Woodard, take care."

"Okay, bye."

I got dressed, said a quick prayer, and then left out to
go to work. Driving to work I kept having flashbacks
of Marcus and our abusive relationship. I saw how
Marcus dragged me from my bedroom into my living
room kicking me in my ribs. I snapped out of my daze
and focused on the road. I kept looking in the
rearview and side mirrors like he was on the road with
me. Finally I pulled in the garage at work. Going to my
cubicle, I was still a little uneasy, looking around

before I sat down. It took me a minute before I was able to focus and get my work started.

Later that day I was getting off work and I went to the super market to grab a few things. Dragging my cart down the bread aisle, there was a guy that touched me from behind. I was pissed when I spoke, "What the hell." When I turned around and looked up, it was Lay. My heart skipped a beat because I was so surprised to see him. I could never tire of those gorgeous brown eyes and that wonderful smile.

"How you doing, Miss Lady?" he said leaning against the shelf.

"Lay," I said, trying to sound disinterested.

"Oh it's like that?" he said flashing his smile again.

"Sure is. Where is the raw meat that you left me for?"

"We broke up."

"Umm, that grass wasn't so green on the other side now was it?" I said trying to push his buttons.

"You could say that. It's funny, Mel, 'cause I have been thinking about you lately."

"I just know you weren't. I'm only the friend, remember?"

"Yes, but that's what I thought you were until I left, and now I know you are more than a friend to me,

Mel."

"You would say that now it didn't work out with you and Olive Oil."

"Just have dinner with me, one time please," he said holding his hands as if he was praying.

"I guess I could do that, and it will give me a chance to cuss you out more."

"You're funny, Mel."

"I'm not laughin'."

We exchanged numbers and as I left the store I didn't know whether to be happy or be pissed off.

I was sitting at the table in Olive Garden waiting for Lay. I glanced at my watch and noticed that he was ten minutes late. Sipping on my wine, I thought, Five more minutes and I'm out. Five minutes had passed and I was just about to ask for the check from the waiter when Lay walked up to the table with a bundle of roses in his hand.

"These are for you."

"Gee, thanks. You must really think you getting some tonight, huh."

"Come on, Mel, it's been a year since we broke up and you think I'm trying to get some?"

"That's what I said, I didn't stutter."

"You are really going to be hard on me, aren't you? I mean I know I deserve it, but damn."

"So you wanted to have dinner to talk, so talk, my soaps come on in an hour and my V8 is waiting on me in the fridge."

"Well...I....Mel, I love you and I made a mistake leaving you and I would like to pick up where we left off."

I wanted to kick my own ass for getting emotional, but it bubbled in me as I asked, "Why, so you can leave me again for another woman?"

"I know I made a mistake and you are the only woman that is good for me. Mel, I was stupid for ever leaving you." I saw the waiter at another table and got his attention.

"Uh, could I have another glass of wine, matter a fact bring the whole bottle please."

"Yes, Ma'am." The waiter said.

"Lay, you mean to tell me that you want me back after you left me for another woman and I'm supposed to obey your wishes like I'm a fucking dog?"

"No, Mel, that's not what I'm saying."

"No, I know exactly what you are saying. Do you have any idea what you put me through since I met you?

You have caused me so much emotional pain that
when men ask me out I'm afraid to date them because
I think they will leave me for another woman!" I
started to cry and Lay got up from the chair to console
me.

"Don't touch me."

"Mel, let me hold you."

"I said don't touch me."

The waiter came and sat the bottle down on the table.
He sensed the tension and was off as quick as he
came. I finished another glass of wine in one gulp and
started to fill tipsy.

"I can't do this, Lay, I have to go. I thought that I
would be strong enough, but I can't do this."

"Okay then we won't. We will talk about it some other
time."

"Waiter, please bring the check," I said so I could
finally leave.

"Yes, Ma'am."

"I'll pay for the check, Mel."

"Okay," I said knowing the more time I spent around
Lay the weaker I would get.

I went to get up from the chair, and I almost fell until
Lay caught me.

"Are you okay?"

"Why do you care? I need my keys so that I can go."

"Mel, I don't want you driving in your condition, I'll take you home."

"You would just love that wouldn't you?" I said clearly tipsy.

Lay walked me outside to his car.

"Uh, I drove my car here."

"I know. We will get it in the morning."

"What the hell is this we shit, nucca? You ain't back."

"Fine, we will drive your car, and I will catch a bus to get mine tomorrow. Damn, you are so fucking stubborn."

During the drive home I fell asleep in the car. Lay carried me into the house and put me in the bed. I was sleep for a good three hours when I jumped up from the dream I was having about Marcus trying to kill me.

"Lay!"

"I'm right here, Mel. What's wrong?"

"Just hold me please."

Lay held me tight and we started kissing passionately. I held back because I told myself that he would never have me again. Then he whispered in my ear, "Baby, its okay. I love you." We made love the entire night until we fell into a deep sleep. The next morning I woke up to breakfast in bed: eggs, pancakes, and turkey bacon. While I was in the bed eating, my phone rang and it startled me.

"Hello."

"Daughter, what you doing?"

"Hey mom, I'm just sitting here eating breakfast."

"You sound funny wit the way you talking, who's with you?"

"You wouldn't believe me if I told you."

"Tell Lay I said hi, and it's about time."

"Mom, how did you know?"

"What? Did you think y'all met in a supermarket by coincidence?"

"Wow, you are so wack for that one!" I said laughing.

"Well even though he was an asshole, he makes you happy and despite all his bullshit I want my daughter to be happy."

"Goodbye, Mom, I love you and I'll call you later."

Lay was on the bed smiling from ear to ear. Then my phone rang again.

"Hello."

"Yes, is Miss Woodard available?"

"This is she."

"Miss Woodard, Marcus is on the run and he has a capius out on him. Should you see or have contact with him, please call 911 right away."

"Is there any way you can send a patrol car over here?"

"Yes, ma'am, we'll be in touch."

"Marcus fucking with you again?" Lay said with anger resonating in his voice.

"Yup, it started yesterday."

"I ain't gonna let him hurt you, you know that right?" Lay said, wrapping his arms around me.

"Yes," I said feeling safe in his embrace.

THREE MONTHS LATER

It was a Saturday afternoon and I was ready to pick up the engagement ring from the jewelry store. When I got inside, the salesman said, "Melanie?"

"Yes," I said recognizing him.

"Your order is ready. Now are you sure that size 9 is right?"

"Yes."

"Melanie, I have got to say this ring is gorgeous and it is very rare for the women to propose to the man, but it's still so romantic."

"Thank you, Oscar, is it?"

"Yes, ma'am."

"Thanks, Oscar, I think I am ready for this."

"You'll be fine," he said with a wave of the hand.

I grabbed the bag and headed home to pop the big question. Why was I so nervous? What if he said no and left me again for another woman? I snapped out of my crazy thoughts and pulled up to my house. Lay's car was parked outside. Even though I was going to propose marriage to him I had another surprise that shocked me but would really shock him, and I didn't know how he would take it. I entered the door and

Lay was on the couch watching the game.

"Lay, I want to cook a special dinner for us tonight."

"Aawww, baby, I cooked dinner already. Look at the table. I was just waiting for you."

"Okay, well then let's eat and I want to ask you something."

"Should I be worried?"

"No silly."

We sat at the table and Lay had prepared spaghetti and salad for us, and boy I loved his spaghetti. When we were finished eating I grabbed the bag.

"Lay, we have had our ups and our downs and I remember the day before my grandmother died she said that I wouldn't see the last of you. Well I still haven't seen the last of you years later. I have forgiven you and I'm ready to move on to the next step." I grabbed the box out the bag and opened the box, then I got on one knee and said, "Lay Bryant, will you marry me?"

He sat there looking at me awkwardly then smiled and said, "Mel, I thought I was supposed to ask you, but baby, yes I will. I love you so much, Melanie. I didn't see it then, but I see it now. You are my soul mate."

He was quiet for a moment before adding, "I also have

something to tell you."

"Oh God, what is it?" I said laughing.

"While we were separated, I wanted you back so bad. The only way I knew we would be happy was to get my vasectomy reversed, and I saved the money for it and I did it. The doctor said that I was able to make babies again."

Tears started rolling down my cheeks. They were finally tears of joy for a change.

"Lay, are you serious?"

"Yes, baby, I am."

"I'm so glad to hear that. Can you reach in the bag? There is another gift for you."

Lay reached in the bag and pulled out a pregnancy test box.

Lay had an awkward look on his face. Then the awkwardness turned to excitement and he began to get emotional.

I smirked and said, "Open it up now."

When he opened the box, he pulled out the test and saw two plus signs.

His eyes widened to the size of saucers. "Baby, stop playing. Is this for real?"

I nodded. "It sure is."

He was so excited that he kissed me and picked me up
at the same time.

"Baby, I didn't know."

"Me either until this afternoon," I said, smiling.

Lay called his family and told them the good news and
I did the same. Now we had to get started on re-
planning our wedding. I couldn't wait to marry Lay.

*****

It was the day of our wedding and I was scared
shitless. We were having just close family at the
wedding and then a huge reception. Money was tight
with the baby coming and all. I had on an egg shell
white wedding dress that flared out at the bottom.
Lay's mother and Jackie were helping me with the
dress.

"Mother in law, you were right. This dress is perfect."

"I told you, Mel, and it has enough room for you and
my grand baby."

"Mom, can you fix my veil, please?"

"Mel, you are beautiful," Jackie said as she adjusted
the veil.

"Thanks, Mom."

After I was done getting into my dress, I walked out of
the room surprised at the sight in front of me. My dad

showed up to walk me down the aisle, although he was against me marrying Lay.

"Daddy, I thought you weren't coming."

"I only have one daughter and I love you too much to miss your day."

"Awww thank you, Daddy."

"Oh, Melanie, you look so beautiful, Shug would have loved to see this," Eryca said as she walked in.

"Eryca, this is my wedding day. I don't want to ruin my make up just yet."

"Okay girl, I was looking for the bathroom. I didn't even mean to come in here but now that I did I just had to tell you that."

Eryca and everyone else left the room except me and my dad.

"Boop, you sure you want to do this?" he asked. "You know Daddy parked his car out back just in case you changed your mind."

"Dad, I love Lay and I know he loves me," I said with confidence.

"Okay then, just don't have my grandson here at the church," he said, smiling.

"Five more months to go Dad." I hit his shoulder.

The music stared playing and I could feel the tears

starting. My dad and I walked out and everyone had their eyes on us. I couldn't believe that I was actually getting married. After all I had been through with men, I never thought I was worthy of being a wife. I just stared at Lay as I walked down the aisle, and he looked so sexy in his black tuxedo. The music stopped playing and Lay and I joined hands. He was smiling at me and I was so excited.

"Dearly beloved," the pastor began, "we are gathered here today to celebrate this happy couple Melanie Woodard and Lay Bryant." The baby was kicking which made me grab my stomach. The pastor asked me, "Melanie, are you okay?"

"Yes, I'm sorry. The baby is just kicking a lot." Everyone started laughing.

The pastor continued, "If anyone can show cause why this couple should not be married, speak now or forever hold your piece." Lay and I both looked around and we started laughing along with everyone else. Then the pastor said, "Who gives this woman away to this man?"

I was so embarrassed because my entire family stood and said "We do." It was so cute and funny at the same time. We then exchanged vows and we were announced husband and wife. During our kiss, we heard a loud commotion coming from outside of the church. All of a sudden, the doors swung open and Marcus bust in the church, pointing a gun right at me.

"Marcus, please don't hurt anybody!" I said trembling.

"If anybody moves, I'll shoot her right now," he said, keeping the gun aimed at me.

"Melanie, if I can't have you, no one will. Bitch, you dying today!"

Lay pushed me out the way and that's when I heard the gun go off. Everyone in the church was screaming and my dad was looking for Marcus. When I looked down, Lay had been shot in the chest.

"Oh my God, oh my God. Lay get up, open your eyes. Breathe baby, please breathe." Lay was lying there in his own blood. Jackie used to be a nurse, so she came to Lay and checked for a pulse to see if he was breathing. She was crying hysterically, "Oh my God, he's not breathing, he's not breathing." I don't know who called the paramedics, but they showed up and put Lay on a gurney. "Will he make it?" I said as the tears fell harder.

"Ma'am we have to get him a hospital."

I hugged Lillian and we both were crying. Everyone

was following the paramedics to the hospital when we heard another gun shot. Marcus had shot himself in the foot trying to get away. My dad, Q, and Blair all chased him in hopes of whooping his ass.

EPILOUGE

By the grace of god Lay survived the gunshot wound to his chest. There was no permanent damage and he was able to make a full recovery. Our daughter Kashya Lynn Bryant was a healthy girl weighing in at six pounds. We are still married happily. As for Marcus, well my dad and cousins beat him pretty badly. He got fifteen to life in prison for attempted murder in the second degree.

After having Kashya, I received my bachelor's degree in psychology. I finally could say that I was happy. I had the man of my dreams, my bachelor's degree, and the most beautiful little girl in the world. Jackie even started going to rehab. I know Shug would have been proud to see what my life had become. Like I said, I knew I was here for a purpose and for the first time I was truly living.